A Trail of Echoes

Echoes

A Shade of Vampire, Book 18

Bella Forrest

ALSO BY BELLA FORREST:

A SHADE OF VAMPIRE SERIES:

Derek & Sofia's story:

A Shade of Vampire (Book 1)
A Shade of Blood (Book 2)
A Castle of Sand (Book 3)
A Shadow of Light (Book 4)
A Blaze of Sun (Book 5)
A Gate of Night (Book 6)
A Break of Day (Book 7)

Rose & Caleb's story:

A Shade of Novak (Book 8)
A Bond of Blood (Book 9)
A Spell of Time (Book 10)
A Chase of Prey (Book 11)
A Shade of Doubt (Book 12)
A Turn of Tides (Book 13)
A Dawn of Strength (Book 14)
A Fall of Secrets (Book 15)
An End of Night (Book 16)

The Shade lives on…

A Wind of Change (Book 17)
A Trail of Echoes (Book 18)

A SHADE OF KIEV TRILOGY:

A Shade of Kiev 1
A Shade of Kiev 2
A Shade of Kiev 3

BEAUTIFUL MONSTER DUOLOGY:

Beautiful Monster 1
Beautiful Monster 2

For an updated list of Bella's books,
please visit www.bellaforrest.net

Contents

CHAPTER 1: RIVER

I glanced up at Benjamin Novak across the bare-walled guest room. The shock of being told that I was now immortal had not yet passed, but my mind was filled with one thought. I had to find a way to turn myself back and return to my family. And I had to do it soon. Each hour that passed, anxiety gripped me more and more at the thought of how distraught my family must be.

Ben met my eyes.

"Where is The Shade?" I asked.

"In the Pacific Ocean."

My heart sank. "The Pacific Ocean? But that's like... halfway across the globe. How on earth am I going to get there? I have no passport..."

"We're going to have to travel by boat."

"We?"

Ben frowned. "Yes. We. I said that I would help you get to The Shade."

"Oh," I said, staring at him. "I didn't think that you were actually going to take me there. I thought you said that you want to stay away—"

"I can help you get there without actually setting foot on the island. Besides, if I didn't accompany you there, there's no way in hell you would find it. Trust me."

Again, I couldn't help but wonder why he was doing this for me. Although he said that he wouldn't feel right leaving me stranded on my own, taking me all the way to the Pacific Ocean was putting himself out in a massive way.

And so I asked him again, "Ben, why would you do this for me?"

He breathed out. "Well, I suppose it's not entirely selfless. You could act as a messenger for me, let my family know that I'm still alive and intend to return as soon as I feel able to. I haven't contacted them since I left."

"How come? Can't you just phone them?"

He shook his head. "There's a spell cast over the island so only charmed phones will work. I was in such a hurry to leave the place, stupidly, I left the island without one." He leaned back on his bed. "Anyway, even traveling by ship, I'm not sure how we're going to pull this off. But the first thing we ought to do is convert some coins into cash. God knows how much money we're wasting by dishing those out. When we leave this evening, our first stop should be a pawnbroker."

I picked up my bag, heavy with coins, and looked at them again. I had no idea how much they were worth. We would soon find out. As I reached inside, my fingers brushed against the cool glass of the vial of amber liquid I'd been given while in Michael's quarters. I lifted it up and examined it once again, trying to guess what on earth it was. How did they even know about my brother and why would they give him a gift?

Staring at it wasn't going to get me any closer to an answer, so I slipped it back in the bag and looked back at Ben.

"It's going to be a long night," he said. "I suggest you get some rest."

"I guess you're right."

Once we left this guesthouse, we didn't know when we would find our next shelter. And we needed to be alert now more than ever.

I placed my backpack on the floor and swung my legs onto my bed. Gathering my blanket, and the one that Ben had given me, I rested my head against my stiff pillow and watched as Ben lay down on his own bed. He faced the wall, turning his back on me.

I closed my eyes, and it was only once I did that I realized just how heavy my eyelids felt. Every limb in my body felt exhausted and torn from the trauma I had just endured. And yet, after half an hour, I still had not fallen asleep. My mind simply wouldn't shut down as worry after worry continued to flood my head. I couldn't stop thinking about my family and if I was ever going to make it back to them. I kept thinking about how worried they would all be. Especially my mother.

I sat up in bed.

It might not be safe for me to visit my grandfather's house, but at least I could try to speak to him on the phone to ease my family's stress. Once Ben and I left Cairo, especially if we were going to be traveling by sea, we would soon have no access to payphones.

I looked over toward Ben. His back heaved slightly, and his breathing was slow and steady. Clearly he had managed to fall asleep. Touching my feet to the ground, I stood up.

I had no idea how long he would remain asleep, but I couldn't lie awake in the silence of this room any longer, tortured by my own thoughts.

Grabbing a small notepad from the dressing table between the twin beds, I scribbled a note for Ben explaining where I had gone and that I would aim to be back within an hour. Judging by how soundly he appeared to be sleeping, I doubted he would wake up before I returned.

Picking up my backpack, I moved toward the door. But just before I opened it, I had second thoughts. I didn't *think* that he was going to wake up before I returned, but just in case he did…

I reached for the empty water bottle I'd placed by the doorway and carried it into the bathroom. I looked around for a sharp object. Ben's claws would be useful about now. The edge of the mirror looked quite sharp—it was poorly made and didn't even have a frame to cover the glass. It was just rectangularly cut and stuck straight on the wall. Raising my wrist toward it, I hoped that I wouldn't contract some kind of infection as I cut myself with it. Biting my lip against the pain, I allowed my blood to trickle into the bottle. Once I felt that there was enough, I screwed on the cap and placed it on the bedside table next to the note.

And then I left the room. Before I could make any calls, I needed cash. That meant a trip to a pawnbroker first. I supposed if I asked at the reception desk to use the phone, they would let me, but I couldn't afford to be overheard. I needed to reach a pay phone.

The same man who'd checked us in was sitting behind the desk. He looked up as I approached.

"Is the room to your liking?" he asked.

"It's fine," I said. "I came to ask you if there are any pawnbrokers near here?"

"Hmm. That depends on what you mean by 'near'. There are several, but they are situated more centrally."

"Distance is not a problem," I said. "Could you please write down the address of the nearest one, and would you also have a map?"

"Yes," he said, eyeing me curiously. He reached beneath his desk and pulled out a blank piece of paper, and a map of Cairo. Once he had written the address on the paper, he drew an "X" on the map where the street was located.

"Thank you." I said, taking both items from him. I studied the map as I exited the guesthouse. I could run so fast now, I guessed that it would take me less than half an hour to reach the destination. Assuming things went smoothly at the pawnbroker and I managed to find a pay phone, I would be back in no time.

I tucked the map and the piece of paper into the deep pockets of my robe and tightened my shoes before launching into a sprint. I kept referring to the map every now and then, stopping to check street names.

I ran so fast, I arrived in fifteen minutes. I wasn't even breathless either.

I looked up at the signpost of the shop. *Cleopatra Jewelers*. Adjusting my veil, which had gotten a little askew during my running, I looked down at the wound I'd caused by cutting myself. It had almost entirely healed by now.

I stepped into the shop. I was the only customer, which I was thankful for, and there was just one employee sitting behind the counter. I walked up to him and placed my backpack on the table. I undid the zipper and pulled out just a handful of the gold coins.

I explained to him in Arabic that I wanted to sell the gold for cash. His eyes widened a little as I handed him the precious metal. I tried to wait patiently as he went about examining the gold, until finally, about half an hour later, I was walking out of the shop with a backpack stuffed with cash. It was so full, the zipper was close to breaking.

The first thing I had to do was buy a new bag. I found a bag shop in the second street along and, once I had chosen a bag and paid for it, I placed my backpack inside the larger one, then put that on my back instead.

After only five minutes of searching, I managed to locate a phone box. My hand was shaking as I reached for the receiver and inserted a coin. My heart pounding, I dialed my grandfather's number and clutched the phone to my ear.

Ring. Ring.

Ring. Ring.

Come on, Grandpa. Pick up.

When the phone kept ringing and eventually reached voicemail, I hung up and tried to call again after waiting a minute. The phone continued to ring with no answer. This time I left a message.

"G-Grandpa, this is River. I hope you've been reunited with Lalia by now. I'm calling to tell you that I'm fine. I can't say much, and I can't tell you where I am, but I'm going to try to make it back to you, or back to Mom, as soon as I can. Please just try not to worry about me. I'm… I'm in safe hands. Sending my love to you, Lalia, Dafne, Jamil and Mom."

I placed the phone back on the receiver, exhaling deeply. It felt like some of the weight on my chest had lifted. I hoped my grandfather would check his voicemail soon.

Backing away from the phone box, I began to hurry back along the winding streets toward our guesthouse. When I entered the reception area, there was no one sitting behind the desk. I headed for the staircase and ran, moving quickly along the corridor upstairs until I reached the room.

I was about to knock on the door when I noticed that it was ajar.

Pushing it open, I looked around.

Ben's bed was empty, as was the rest of the room.

Ben was gone.

CHAPTER 2: RIVER

I rushed to the bathroom. That too was empty. My mouth became parched as my eyes fixed on the dressing table. The note and the bottle of my blood still sat on the table, untouched.

Fear gripped me as doubts began to flood my mind. *Where is he? Did he change his mind and just leave without me?*

A bloodcurdling scream stopped me short. It came from downstairs. Panic coursing through my veins, I shot out of the room and hurried back down the stairs.

The screaming continued. It was coming from the room behind the empty reception desk. Racing around it, I forced the door open and barged in.

It was all I could do to not scream too.

The room looked like a scene out of a horror movie. The bodies of three men lay strewn about the room, one of whom I recognized as the man who'd sat at the desk. There were deep puncture marks in their necks, their bodies splattered with blood.

And in the far right corner of the room, Ben was sucking the life from a young woman before my very eyes. His hips crushed against her thin frame, holding her in place against the wall as he took deep gulps of her blood.

"No!" I croaked. "Ben!"

I threw myself across the room at him, sliding my arms around his neck and pulling myself up onto his back. Holding him in a choke, I tried to force him to release the girl. That was not the wisest idea though because even if I managed to pull him away, his fangs would rip through her jugular. Instead, I placed one palm over his forehead, holding his head steady, then positioned my right wrist directly beneath his nose.

"Let her go," I begged, whispering into his ear. His eyes narrowed, and I could feel shudders passing through his body as he drank. But then the scent of my blood, so close to him, began to take its effect. Apparently I smelled so disgusting that I was spoiling his appetite. After four more gulps, his jaw loosened, and he released the girl.

Her face was frozen in utter terror as she collapsed on the floor.

Afraid to step away from Ben in case he launched another attack, I pulled him down to the floor with me as I checked the girl's pulse. It was so faint, I could barely feel it.

"You need to heal her with your blood," I hissed to Ben, having no idea whether vampire blood could even heal a person at such a desperate stage.

He still seemed to be in a daze, his whole face now contorted with some kind of pain of his own.

"Ben! Give her your blood."

Extending a claw, he cut his palm and held it to the girl's lips.

"Drink," I urged, clutching the girl by the shoulder. But she didn't.

I shook her hard. But as I checked her pulse again, it became clear that I could shake her until her neck came loose. She wasn't going to respond. She was gone, as gone as the other ravaged corpses in this room.

Standing up with Ben, I placed both palms against his chest and pushed him back against the wall.

"What the hell were you thinking?" I asked through trembling lips. "I left my blood for you!"

Ben's eyes looked unfocused, blood still dripping from his lips, onto his soaked robe. His voice was low and hoarse as he responded. "You shouldn't have left without warning me."

Ding! Ding!

The shrill sound of the bell at the front desk pierced the atmosphere.

My hair stood on end. I looked in panic from Ben to the corpses scattered around the room.

"Excuse me," a high-pitched voice called in Arabic. "Excuse me!"

Shooting to the door, and wiping the blood that had

14

gotten on me onto my black robe on the way, I stepped out of the room and back into the reception area, closing the door behind me and standing there, holding the handle in place. Now that I had distanced myself from Ben again, I was half expecting him to storm out and attack the middle-aged Arab woman standing behind the desk.

"What was all that screaming?" the woman complained, her black eyebrows knotting. "It woke me from my rest."

"Oh, I'm so sorry, ma'am," I replied, trying to act as though I had just returned from a toilet break rather than from witnessing a bloody massacre. "It was coming from the street outside. I am not certain what happened, since I have been busy with paperwork."

"Hm." The woman eyed me curiously, then her expression turned back to annoyance. "Anyway, I also came down to tell you that the flush in my toilet has stopped working."

"Oh, dear. That is… entirely unacceptable. If you return to your room now, I will send someone up in the next hour. Okay?"

"In the next hour? I can't wait that long!" she grumbled.

"Okay," I replied. "How about in the next fifteen minutes? I will try to get hold of our caretaker."

She still looked dissatisfied, but to my relief, she headed back up the staircase.

I clutched the door handle and stepped back inside the room, slamming the door behind me.

My stomach lurched as I looked over the horrifying scene once again. I half expected Ben to be crouching over the girl, drawing out the very last drops of blood from her still-warm corpse. But no. He was sitting on the floor in the far corner of the room, his back against the wall, his head clutched in his hands, breathing heavily.

I hurried over to him and bent down to his level, gripping his shoulders.

"Ben," I rasped. "We have to leave. If someone finds us…" I looked up at the ceiling. If there were any surveillance cameras in here, they were well hidden because I couldn't spot any.

"Get up," I urged.

When he looked at me, his green eyes seemed darker than usual. Much darker. They were practically black.

His mouth was no longer covered in blood. I could see that he'd wiped it against his sleeve. He stood up, slightly unsteady. His jaw clenched as he eyed the corpse nearest to us.

"Let's get out of here," he said. He reached for my wrist and closed his hand around it. The next thing I knew, he was pulling me into the reception area and out of the main exit of the guesthouse. When we arrived on the street outside, it was dark. He gathered me onto his back and lurched forward with speed that made my stomach flip.

I was still feeling overwhelmed at what I'd just witnessed Ben do. I'd known that he was a vampire, but I'd never witnessed such a harrowing scene, even during my stay at The Oasis. And Ben... although he had told me about his struggle around humans, I'd still thought he was different because of the way he'd treated me. Seeing his darkness so starkly before me was something that I was still trying to come to terms with.

As he ran, we were just a blur in the darkness. It was a good thing too. Although he was wearing black, which helped to camouflage the stains, his robe was drenched in blood. We were moving too fast to see, but I was certain that we were leaving traces of blood on the sidewalk.

My grip around Ben's shoulders tightened.

"We have to stop and get you some new clothes," I said.

He didn't argue with me. I was sure that he was having the same thoughts about leaving a trail behind us. We stopped as we reached a night market and he placed me down on the ground.

Taking the backpack off my shoulders, I dug inside and reached for a few notes—enough for new clothes. I handed the backpack to Ben, who put it on his back. He stood behind me, one arm wrapped around my waist and the other holding my upper left arm as we walked forward. His position against me made me feel like a prisoner being escorted somewhere.

I didn't tempt fate while stopping by a clothes store and made our visit quicker than I'd thought possible. I chose the robe within a matter of seconds, and then thrust the cash at the stall owner, not even waiting for the correct amount of change.

We rushed away from the market and arrived at a quiet road. We stopped at the doorway of an old building. Placing the backpack on the ground, he pulled off his robe, then removed his pants, stripping to his underwear. I was supposed to be keeping watch, but I was embarrassed to find my eyes roaming his ridiculously attractive physique.

I tore my eyes away as he stepped into his fresh pants and pulled on the new robe. Bundling up the old soiled clothes, he threw them into a trashcan at the side of the road and turned back to me.

"Okay," he said quietly. "Let's continue."

"Where to now?" I asked.

"Now, we need to head for water. The Nile. Do you have any idea how to get there? Are we going to need to pick up a map?"

"I have a map," I said, reaching into the backpack. I pulled it out and handed it to Ben.

He opened it up and looked at it. Although it was

dark, and there were no streetlights where we were standing, we could both see all the details of the map clearly. My supernatural vision was yet another thing I was still getting used to.

We found our location on the map, then figured out the quickest route that involved passing by the least number of humans. Once we were confident in the plan, I climbed onto Ben's back, the backpack once again fastened over my shoulders.

Then he ran nonstop, slowing down only occasionally to consult the map he had gripped in his hand to ensure that we were still going in the right direction.

Soon, the night air felt cooler and fresher. I sensed that we were approaching a body of water. When Ben stopped, we were standing in a dark harbor. A myriad of boats surrounded us. There were larger vessels—as large as cruise ships—as well as smaller ones like speedboats.

"So we're going to need to choose a route and buy a ticket?" I asked.

Ben shook his head. "We need to avoid people as

much as possible."

I had already guessed what was on his mind as his eyes settled on a speedboat about fifteen feet away from us.

"Stealing?" I asked in a small voice.

"I don't see what other choice we have right now."

"So you know how to navigate the boat?" I asked.

"I'm used to navigating submarines. I can handle a boat," he muttered. I slid off his back and watched as he looked quickly around the harbor, then leapt onto the boat. I motioned to follow, but he held up a hand.

"Just stay where you are and keep watch. Shout if you see someone coming."

I did as he requested. It seemed to be a quiet evening on the harbor. There weren't many people around at all, making my task an easy one.

About five minutes later the engine chortled and he returned, nodding in my direction.

"Okay. I've figured out how to get the boat to start without keys."

He held out a hand, and I took it as he helped me onto the boat. He led me into the small cockpit in the center of the deck, and we both took a seat. Adjusting the controls, Ben began to navigate the boat backward. As soon as he had maneuvered out of the bay, he ramped up the speed. Soon we'd left the harbor and were moving toward the center of the wide river.

He kept the lights switched off as he looked up and down the river. There were a number of other boats on the water at this time of night. We had to be careful to avoid them because they could not see us.

We sailed north along the river for the next few hours, dodging any boats that passed our way, until the lights along the riverbank began to grow dimmer.

"We're running out of fuel," Ben said. "We're going to have to head for land."

Surrounding us on either side were tall marshes. Clearly we had traveled a good distance away from the city and were in some kind of suburb. Ben navigated the boat toward land and I gripped the sides of the boat as it hit the bank. As we both stepped out, I winced as mud filled my shoes.

He held my hand and we waded through the sludge until we reached a concrete road. There were no other boats nearby along the bank that we could see.

"We should start heading north by foot. It will be faster anyway. The boat was just to get us out of the city." He inhaled deeply. "Definitely not as much human blood around here."

"Good," I muttered.

I decided that I wanted to run for a while, so we raced along the roads of the sleepy suburbs that passed nearest to the river. The chirp of crickets filled my ears, and the occasional roaring of a truck as it trundled by… and then, once we had entered the early hours of the morning, the sound of helicopters slicing the air above us.

Ben and I sped up, trying to keep out of the spotlights that the choppers were shining down, but they kept hovering nearby. I shot a panicked glance at Ben. Gripping my hand, he tugged on me sharply and pulled us into some bushes to our right. As he kept leading me forward, the shrubbery got thicker and thicker and the ground muddier. Ben removed the backpack from his back and hung it over a low-hanging tree branch, then pulled me into the river until I was chest deep.

"Take a deep breath," he whispered.

I didn't have time to draw in much breath before he pulled me under with him. I remained submerged for as long as I could before I was forced to resurface for oxygen. I ducked down quickly again afterward. We remained in the water for what felt like the next ten minutes, until the helicopters seemed to have passed.

We headed back to the bank, where Ben retrieved the backpack from the branch and continued running. As the first light of morning showed behind the horizon, we arrived at a harbor on the outskirts of a small town. Looking around, I was disappointed to see only cruise ships.

"What now?" I asked, looking nervously at the sky.

Ben eyed the huge ships.

"We have two options. Keep traveling by foot and hope we find another boat soon, before the sun rises… or buy tickets on one of these cruise ships."

I stared at him, wondering if the last part was some kind of joke.

"You, on a cruise?"

He looked back at me. "Given the searches on the roads last night, I don't think it's a good idea to travel by land. But we need to keep moving." He averted his eyes to the brightening sky. "Trust me when I say I feel crazy for suggesting this, but I think we're going to be safer in one of those cruise ships, at least until tonight." I gaped at him as he continued. "By my estimation, if we pass the day on a cruise ship along the Nile, of course it will go slow, but then we'll only need one more night of traveling by foot—if that—and we'll end up in Ismailia. There we're sure to find a boat to take us down to the Red Sea, toward the Gulf of Aden, and hopefully as far as the Arabian Sea."

After everything I had seen of Ben's behavior, I was beyond nervous at the idea of him being stuck on a boat surrounded by possibly hundreds of humans. I wouldn't be able to leave his side for a moment.

I gulped, then looked toward the small cabin in the middle of the harbor buildings that, going by the sign above its door, was a ticket office.

"Well, first, let's see if there are even tickets available," I said. "They might be fully booked."

We headed down to the building and I was surprised to see it was open so early. Ben moved close behind me, one arm around my waist as I pushed the door open and we stepped inside.

There was a bleary-eyed Arab man sitting at a desk.

"Hello," he said, forcing a smile.

Ben motioned to take a seat next to me behind the desk, but I sat myself on his lap so that the back of my neck was pressed hard against his face. It was too early in the morning for me to witness another slaughter.

The man raised a brow at me as I looked at him, unfazed.

"Good morning," I replied in Arabic, clearing my throat. "What cruises do you have available today?"

He pulled out a pamphlet from one of the drawers. "There are quite a few leaving and stopping by this port. Where would you like to go?"

"Uh, any ship traveling north or eastward."

He frowned. "That's a little vague, ma'am."

"What is the earliest you have?"

"*The Empress* should be stopping here for a short break in... about fifteen minutes, actually. I might be able to find a spare cabin." He handed me a pamphlet about the cruise and squinted as he eyed his computer.

I glanced through the pamphlet, waiting with bated breath.

"Hm, no... I'm sorry. *The Empress* appears to be fully booked."

"Then when would the next—?"

"Oh, wait." He held up a hand. "Yes, there is a spare cabin. But it's a very expensive one—the executive suite on the top level of the vessel."

"Will it be making any stops this evening, after sunset?"

"One stop at about 9pm, though only a very short one."

"That's fine," I said immediately. "We'll book that."

When the man told me the price, I barely batted an eyelid. We had more than enough.

Daring to shift my weight from Ben for a second, I reached for the backpack and then sat back down again. Reaching into the bag, I counted the cash and handed it to the man. He issued us the tickets and instructed us where to wait. But the sun's rays had begun to trickle down upon the harbor.

Although I was anxious to get Ben far away from this man, I asked, "Would it be possible to wait in here until it comes?"

He nodded. "Do you have any luggage that you need help with?" he asked, looking through the window outside as if wondering if we had left it out there.

"No," I said. "We, uh, travel light."

He raised a brow and then looked back at his computer.

Ben and I waited in tense silence until a large ship came into view and stopped at the edge of the harbor. It ended up being sixteen minutes late. I thanked the ticket agent before Ben and I hurried out of the office and toward one of the nearest entrances of the long boat that had just opened up.

Since it was early in the morning, apart from the man who greeted us at the entrance and gave us our key, we only met a handful of other humans on our way up to our room on the top level of the boat. Of course, human blood surrounded us, and I kept a tight grip on Ben in the hallways.

Arriving at our suite, I closed the door behind us and locked it. Now that Ben was inside, I could breathe a little more easily.

I moved farther into the room with Ben. It was luxuriously decorated with wide tinted windows, filled with traditional Egyptian furniture and a large four-poster bed. There was a dining table for two—upon which was a platter of welcome food—that looked out onto a small balcony.

I glanced at Ben.

He still looked so tense he was clearly in no mood to talk. I eyed the food laid out on the table. Removing my veil, I took a seat and began digging into the food.

Ben sat opposite me and swiveled in his chair to look out of the window, his back to me. We didn't talk at all for the next ten minutes as I stuffed myself. When he did swing back around to face me, he looked disturbed.

"Did you hear that?" he asked, his voice hoarse.

"Hear what?" I asked, swallowing a mouthful of juice.

His eyes narrowed and he seemed to be listening to

something. For all my supernatural hearing, I couldn't understand what Ben had noticed. All I could hear were quite ordinary sounds of the ship and the humans around us.

"That," he replied.

I stared at him. "What?"

He paused again. Then he shook his head.

"I guess it was nothing."

CHAPTER 3: BEN

The sounds echoing in my ears didn't match my surroundings. It was as if invisible walls came down around me, blocking out the sounds of the cruise ship, and all went quiet… but for a few sounds. Chillingly familiar sounds.

The wind sighing above me. The dripping of water. The echoing of footsteps against marble. The distant strumming of an instrument. All these might not have been so peculiar in themselves, and I might have even believed that they were noises from the cruise ship, but then came the dull grinding. The same grinding River and I had heard before we escaped. The sound was unmistakable to me.

It felt like I was back in The Oasis.

And then the noises faded away as suddenly as they had arrived, being replaced with the bustle of my current surroundings. I wasn't sure whether to tell River what I had just experienced, or wait until I had a grasp of what was happening. I had scared her more than enough in the past twenty-four hours, so I decided not to. Just in case what I'd heard, or thought I'd heard, had been my imagination—some strange return to the past. Perhaps the noises were imprinted in my mind due to spending weeks down in that atrium.

"What is it?" she pressed, this time reaching for my forearm.

I shook my head again. "I'm not even sure what I heard."

She frowned at me, then rolled her eyes and returned her attention back to her food. We didn't discuss it again until the noises echoed in my ears for a second time later that evening. They remained in my head much longer than before.

This time, I told her.

"You haven't experienced anything like that?" I asked.

She shook her head, her eyes wide with alarm. "How can you be hearing those noises?"

"I have no idea," I replied.

After we discussed it for the next half-hour, River came up with the theory that I must be manifesting some kind of post-traumatic symptoms from being trapped there. I had my doubts about that, but since I wasn't ready to share any theories of my own, I kept quiet.

During the hours that followed, I kept expecting the sounds to return and surround me again, and from the look on River's face, she was expecting it too. But I did not experience it again.

As we waited, although I kept close to River, I found myself occasionally needing to draw her closer to me, lower my face inches above the curve of her neck and breathe in deeply.

About an hour before sunset, River wanted to rest

on the bed. I didn't have a choice but to lie with her on the mattress. She slid beneath the sheets and bunched up the blankets around her, and then I settled next to her, close enough that her knees almost touched mine but not too close that I might disturb her. I intended to remain in this position until she'd finished resting. I was surprised that she was the one who drew nearer still. Raising her head from the mattress, she shuffled closer to me, and then rested her head against my shoulder.

"I'm scared to let you out of my sight," she muttered. "At least if I'm touching you, I'll notice if you slip away."

She was right, of course. I was still a wild animal around human blood. The closer I was to her, the better. I just hadn't wanted to overstep a boundary by moving nearer to her myself. Now that she had broached it, I slid an arm around her and rested my hand against her hip.

"I think you'll definitely notice if I slip away now."

She chuckled, then closed her eyes, apparently comforted by my gesture. My chin resting against the top of her head, I could feel her breathing grow deeper and steadier, until finally she was asleep.

I remained still, careful not to wake her as I looked out of the window, watching the river bank.

Once the boat began to slow, it was time for us to move on. I looked down at River's face. She had an expression of serenity, her pillowy lips flushed. I paused for a moment to admire her beauty, then removed my hand from her hip and brushed her shoulder. When she still didn't stir, I shook her gently.

Her eyelids flickered open, her turquoise gaze fixing on me through her long dark lashes.

"Hmm?"

"The boat's stopping."

She shivered a little as she pushed the blankets away from her, and then stood up. Her eyes were distant as she brushed a hand over her forehead and swayed slightly on the spot. She looked in a daze.

"I had a… strange dream," she said, furrowing her brows.

"What?"

"My mother, two sisters and brother were in it.

They had moved to a pretty part of Manhattan, and were living in a nice apartment. And my brother... He's nineteen and severely autistic, but in the dream, I... I had an actual conversation with him for the first time in my life."

Her words hung in the air as she continued standing, lost in her own thoughts. Then she shook herself and snapped out of it. She walked to the table, poured herself a glass of water, and downed it. Then she took my hand and we moved toward the balcony and looked out. The boat had almost stopped and there was a small harbor nearby.

"Let's go," I said.

River looked at me nervously as I led her to the door.

There was hardly anything I could say to comfort her when I was a bag of nerves myself. I swallowed hard, my mouth watering just at the thought of passing by a human in the corridor. Clenching my jaw, I swung the door open and we stepped outside.

To my anguish, we passed many more humans on the way down than we had on the way up. It was early in the evening, and the ship had come alive with people going to dinner and heading up to the deck to participate in the nighttime entertainment.

River gripped me so hard, if she'd had claws, they would've pierced right through my flesh. But thanks to River's conscientiousness, we made it off the ship and onto the jetty without any bloodshed.

CHAPTER 4: RIVER

As soon as our feet hit the ground, we hurried across the harbor toward a tourist shop. We stopped here to buy another, more detailed map of the area, and then we made our way toward the nearest road. This time, I didn't run. I allowed Ben to carry me, which meant that we moved a lot faster. Racing partly on the road, and partly through the desert, he carried me through the late hours of the night until we ended up in a harbor in Ismailia. I was relieved that we hadn't got caught out in the desert when the sun rose without any shelter for Ben, but it also meant that nobody was around, so we'd have no choice but to take another boat.

Ben chose a vessel that was much larger and sturdier than the speedboat we'd found before, and equipped with lots of extra fuel. I headed below deck to have a look around while Ben figured out how to start the boat. As soon as the engine stuttered and the boat moved forward, I froze.

Footsteps sounded outside, and then three guttural voices shouted in Arabic at once.

"Hey! Stop!"

I shot back up to the deck to see three men dressed in uniform racing toward us carrying guns.

Oh, crap. Security.

I hurried toward Ben, who'd poked his head out of the control room at the commotion. On eyeing the men, he looked ready to pounce. I stood in front of him, blocking his view of the men as they each boarded jet skis and began speeding toward us.

"Just keep the boat moving," I called back to Ben. "I'll try to… deal with this."

Even as Ben ramped up the speed, the men were quickly gaining on us.

Guns began firing as they continued to yell and demand that we stop.

If we ignored them any longer, they'd catch up with the boat and try to board it. And then they'd be directly within Ben's reach.

I rushed down the stairs to the storage room beneath the deck and looked around frantically. I was relieved when I found what I'd hoped to see—a weapon. A rifle to be precise. Grabbing it, I made my way back up to the deck.

I had only practiced using a gun once before in my life, and it was nothing this large, but I didn't have time to doubt myself. As I arrived back on the deck, I ducked down and crawled toward the edge of the boat. I sensed them only feet away now.

I didn't want to harm these people. But we needed to get them off our tail.

Using all the speed that I possessed, I raised myself and began firing wildly over their heads. I was scared that I might actually hit one of them because my hands were so unsteady, but thankfully, my idea ended up working. Having no cover at all, the men had no choice but to fall back and return to shore.

Thank God.

As I made my way back to the front of the boat where Ben was, my hands were still shaking. I sat next to Ben and looked at him. His eyes were set forward, fixed in concentration.

Then he eyed the gun I was holding, and raised a brow. "Did you kill them?"

"No. I could have just let them climb aboard and come near you if I'd wanted to do that… I just scared them off."

Leaning the rifle against the dashboard, I put thoughts of the men aside.

"So now we're headed for the Red Sea," I said. "Do you think this boat will last us?"

"I hope so."

I hoped so too, because I really didn't fancy stopping by another port to meet with more security personnel. Or stealing another boat for that matter.

I tried not to think too much about it, and instead

just focused on the immediate stretch of journey ahead of us.

I leaned back against the wall, and to my annoyance, started shivering again. This coldness was really becoming tiresome. It wasn't even cold outside.

I left Ben and went back down to the lower deck. I entered the bedroom—a small, basic room that could have done with a good refurbishment. But at least it was clean. I tore off the blanket from the double bed and wrapped it around my shoulders before leaving the room and heading back up to join Ben in the control room.

But as I climbed the stairs, I stopped short.

Noises filled my ears—noises that didn't belong on this boat. The echoing of footsteps, the dripping of water, the murmuring of people talking around me, the sound of… grinding.

My tattoo prickled uncomfortably.

I scrambled up the steps and ran toward Ben. He looked at me in surprise as I clutched his shoulders.

"I hear it," I said, my eyes wide. "I hear what you hear. It's like… It's like we never left."

CHAPTER 5: RIVER

After the noises disappeared a few minutes later, I was surrounded again by the sound of water lapping against the boat.

My breathing was quick and shallow as the prickling in my arm began to subside. Looking down at the skin around the etching, I could've sworn that it was glowing with a slight tinge of red.

My hands were trembling.

I'd been alarmed when Ben had told me about it, but experiencing it for myself was an entirely different matter.

I'd thought that perhaps he was just suffering from trauma. But what was the likelihood of me experiencing exactly the same symptoms?

Something else was at work here, and the unknown was terrifying.

Clutching the blanket close to me, I sat next to Ben as he navigated the boat. After a couple of hours, he put it on autopilot and we both went to sit beneath a small shelter on the deck.

By now we had exhausted the topic of what could be happening to us, so I changed the subject.

"So, um, what's it like in The Shade?" I asked, trying to fix my mind on more positive things.

Ben cleared his throat. "Dark. It's forever night there."

I stared at him. "Seriously?"

"Yes, we have witches who've cast a spell on the island—a spell that also makes it invisible to everyone."

"A-and it's full of vampires?"

"Vampires, werewolves, some witches—even an ogre."

"An ogre?"

"As I said, it's a refuge for supernaturals."

Still taking in his words, I looked down at my feet, drawing my knees up to my chest and holding them tight against me.

I wondered if someone there really would be able to cure me. Whether I would be able to return to my family without fear of being hunted down. Whether I could ever live a normal life again, or if that had been snatched from me forever.

Ben shifted in his seat, looking uncomfortable.

"What's wrong?" I asked.

"Hunger pangs," he said, rolling his eyes. "The smell of all those humans really brought my appetite to the surface."

I'd expected that the amount of blood he'd consumed would last much longer. If he was feeling hungry now, when we had only just started out on our journey, God knew what state he would be in when we arrived.

"How will you manage?" I asked.

"I'll figure something out," he said grimly.

I stood up, keeping the blanket around me, and walked out from under the shelter and into the sun.

I faced directly toward it, its rays upon my skin. I closed my eyes and relished the warmth. I didn't feel pain from the sun as vampires did. But perhaps I would if I stayed in it long enough.

I walked to the edge of the boat and leaned my back against the railing, soaking up the sun from this angle while Ben remained in the shade.

I found myself stealing glances at him from across the deck, averting my gaze each time I sensed that he was about to look my way.

The sky began to darken. I looked upward to see a cloud had formed in what had previously been a blue sky. It blocked out the sun and cast a shadow over the boat and the surrounding waters.

I felt a drop of rain fall upon my cheek. The water was cool, and oddly thick. I brushed it aside with the back of my hand.

"Wha—What is that?" Ben said, staring at me.

"What?"

He shot to his feet and closed the distance between

us. He was gazing down at me, a look of disbelief in his eyes. His thumb brushed against my skin where the drop had fallen, and when he lifted it again, it was tinged with red.

I looked down at the back of my hand.

Also stained with red.

I gaped up at the sky, at the cloud above, as droplets fell upon us more rapidly, until a shower of the thick red liquid pounded against the deck.

Blood.

It's raining blood.

CHAPTER 6: BEN

Even as I stared at the blood in horror, my body ached to taste it.

I shook myself, trying to rein in my bloodlust, ashamed that I could be so under its control even at a time like this.

What is happening?

I kept asking myself the question as I stared up at the cloud, squinting through the droplets of blood.

And then I heard it.

A voice, male or female I didn't know. It was too

soft, too echoing, to tell.

It started out quiet, so quiet that I could barely understand what it was saying. Then it grew louder and louder, until it was echoing in my ears so loudly that the words couldn't be mistaken:

"Come back, Benjamin Novak."

My name. How does it know my name?

The resounding voice repeated again and again in some kind of sinister chant. I clutched my ears, as if that would make any difference.

"We know who you are, and we know what you want."

We? Who's we?

I staggered to the edge of the ship, clutching the sides and staring up at the sky, blood now streaming down my face.

Despite my mind being preoccupied, my body was aching for the blood. I reached up to my face, touching the blood, and then moved to taste it.

Human blood.

It's raining human blood.

"Come back, Benjamin Novak…"

Suddenly the tattoo seared severely—more severely

than I remembered experiencing before. My legs gave way beneath me and I fell to the deck, crouched on all fours as I clenched my jaw against the pain.

By my side, River crouched down and touched my shoulder.

I was so consumed by the burning, I could barely see. Then I felt a different type of sensation—a burning not just in my upper arm, but the rest of my body too.

River tugged on me.

"Ben, you need to get out of the sun."

The sun. It had broken through the sky.

The blood stopped. The cloud vanished.

The pain in my tattoo ebbing away, I crawled toward the shelter.

"What's wrong?" River asked, looking at me worriedly.

Still recovering, all I could manage to reply was:

"We need to get you to The Shade."

CHAPTER 7: ROSE

Caleb and I sat on the steps of our mountain cabin, admiring the magnificent view of the island. The ocean in the distance shimmered beneath pale moonlight and a cool breeze rustled the leaves of the redwoods. We planned to move into a new penthouse soon, near the Residences with the other vampires, but for now we were still enjoying this mountain location.

Aside from the strange gray ships moored outside the boundary, things in The Shade had been peaceful since our wedding and the departure of the dragon prince. I wasn't going to complain. We had all had enough drama recently.

I took a sip from my mug of hot chocolate, while Caleb took the last draught from his glass of blood. We sat in silence, content with each other's presence.

I glanced down at the beautiful ring on my finger. It was still bizarre to think that I was married.

Married.

I looked sideways at my new husband. His eyes looked slightly glazed as he looked out toward the ocean in the distance.

"What are you thinking about?" I asked softly, leaning in and resting my head against his shoulder. He wrapped an arm around me, his hand on my thigh as he pulled me closer toward him.

"A lot of things." He averted his eyes away from the ocean and looked down at me, a mischievous glint in his gaze. "One of them being... How much longer do I have to wait for you to finish that hot chocolate so I can take you to bed?"

His gaze gave me butterflies. He hadn't been able to keep his hands off me since we'd exchanged vows.

While previously he had been restrained, he was certainly making up for it now… which sure suited me.

I sloshed the liquid in the cup. It had cooled by now. I swallowed the last two mouthfuls within the space of a few seconds, then showed him the empty cup. "No more need to wonder about that," I said, giving him a sultry look.

His hands reaching around my back and beneath my knees, he swept me up into his arms and carried me back into the cabin. Closing the door behind us, he headed straight for the bedroom and placed me down in the center of the bed. I was expecting him to begin removing his shirt, but instead he paused, giving me a thoughtful look.

"Something else I was thinking about was… our honeymoon," he said.

I raised a brow, moving back toward the headboard and sitting upright. "Oh?"

"I know you said that you don't mind waiting for now, since I'm a vampire and traveling anywhere is going to be difficult. But it doesn't have to be." He reached for the nearby table and slid open the top drawer. He pulled out a sheet of paper filled with sketches and various mathematical notes. It all looked rather complicated, but I focused on the diagram in the center of the paper as he sat next to me and spread the sheet out on the mattress. It was a fairly large boat, about twenty-five feet long and eighteen feet wide according to the notes, and a shelter of some sort covered the entire deck.

"What are you suggesting exactly?" I asked.

"You've never visited New Zealand, have you?"

My pulse quickened in excitement just at the thought. "No."

"Then how about we go on a little tour, stopping by some of the most remote islands in the Pacific Ocean, and make our destination New Zealand?" His brown eyes warmed as he watched my reaction. "This boat is something that I've been working on. Ibrahim would help me to equip it with an exceptionally powerful engine. If it all comes out right, we could stay in the boat by day and at night explore the land."

I couldn't nod more enthusiastically, but there were some things that bothered me about the plan.

He seemed to read my mind and answered my first objection before I even asked it. "Yes, we could just take a submarine, and that way we'd be hidden away from the sun… But we will be spending all the daylight hours on the boat, and we will likely be gone for weeks—there's only so long you can feel comfortable trapped within the hull of a submarine. We'd both be craving the open sea air."

My stomach churned a little. "But what about the hunters?"

"We'll ask Corrine to place a spell over the boat."

"That's while we are at sea, but what about night time, when we reach land?"

"Rose, the places I have in mind to take you to… I doubt we will meet any hunters there. We'll stick to the remote areas and avoid people."

I paused, still uncertain. But the confidence in his expression soon convinced me.

"So"—he moved the plan of the boat aside and leaned in closer to me, his mouth a few inches away from mine—"what do you say, Mrs. Achilles?"

He placed his hands on either side of my hips,

brushing gently against me with his thumbs.

A smile spread across my face. Caleb knew how to melt me.

"Sail away with me, Captain."

CHAPTER 8: ROSE

When I broke the news to my parents about our plan for a honeymoon, they both voiced worries similar to mine about Caleb being a vampire and the threat of the hunters. I let Caleb reassure them in the same way that he had done with me. My father was especially concerned about the hunters because he had been keeping watch on them near the shore. Caleb's words seemed to satisfy my parents for the most part, although my father still seemed tense. I didn't like him to be worried, but I couldn't help but feel warmed on witnessing how genuinely he cared about Caleb's safety. Not so long ago, my father had believed him to be a traitor and tried to kill him.

Now that Caleb and I had made this plan, we didn't want to delay. Caleb finished the boat quickly with the help of Ibrahim, while I took on the task of packing everything I could think of that we might need. Caleb wasn't sure how long it might take us to get to New Zealand, and of course it depended on so many things—how long we decided to spend on each island we stopped at, how rough the weather was, whether we just got lost in each other's eyes in the middle of the ocean for a few days...

The night of our planned departure soon arrived. My parents came early that evening to the cabin, and helped us carry all our baggage to the boat.

When I arrived at the end of the jetty, it was the first time that I had seen the boat completed. It was gorgeous. The covering over the wide deck Caleb had created to give shelter from the sun was made of a dark teak wood, and there was a long sofa in the center with a walnut coffee table, directly in front of the small control room. Beneath the deck were all the amenities we might need—a bedroom with a large window of tinted glass that gave a stunning view of the ocean, an en suite bathroom, a small living room and a storage room equipped with enough supplies to last a month in case of an emergency.

Corrine, Ibrahim, my grandfather, Vivienne and Xavier were waiting for us on the deck. I hugged them each one by one.

"The invisibility and protective spells we've placed over the boat will come into play as soon as you leave The Shade's boundary," Ibrahim said.

"You two be careful," Vivienne murmured, worry in her eyes.

"We will," Caleb said, making his way with a large suitcase toward the staircase leading down to the lower deck.

My parents and I followed him, carrying all the luggage downstairs before returning to say one final goodbye. My mother pulled me close and kissed my cheek.

"Enjoy yourself, sweetheart," she said, squeezing me

tight. "And please… try to stay out of trouble."

"We won't be going anywhere where there's trouble." I chuckled, kissing her back.

I drew away from my mother and wrapped my arms around my father. His hug lifted my feet off the ground.

"Goodbye, darling," he said. "Your mother and I will miss you."

"I'll miss you too," I said, pressing my warm cheek against his.

Then my parents said goodbye to Caleb and stepped back onto the jetty with Vivienne, Xavier, Corrine, Ibrahim, my grandfather and a crowd of people who'd just gathered.

Caleb and I were due to leave now, but we stepped off the boat to say goodbye to the rest of them. Micah was standing—in his wolf form—near the front with his girlfriend, Kira.

"Have a good one," he growled, butting Caleb in the side with his head.

Then he nuzzled my leg.

"Bye, Micah." I ran my fingers through the fur on

his neck and gave him a pat.

Then we spent the next ten minutes saying goodbye to Claudia, Yuri, Anna, Kyle, Griffin, his parents, half a dozen of my girlfriends, and finally, just as we were about to head back toward the boat, I noticed that at the back of the crowd, Jeriad was standing with his girl of choice, Sylvia.

Leaving Caleb, I walked toward the shifter. I was surprised to see him present. I'd hardly seen any of the dragons since my wedding. It was as if they were avoiding me.

He looked at me steadily as I approached.

"Hi, Jeriad," I said, looking from him to Sylvia, whose arm was looped through his.

"I wish you a safe journey," he said, his voice deep and rumbling.

"Thanks," I replied, eyeing him closely. I was about to ask how he and his companions had been, but he didn't give me a chance. Taking Sylvia by the waist, he walked off with her into the woods.

I looked over at Caleb. He raised a brow. I shrugged and made my way back over to him.

"Not sure what's going on with those dragons," I muttered, sliding my hand into his.

We said our final goodbyes and then, clutching the bag of chocolate bunnies Griffin had given me for the journey, I boarded the boat with Caleb. He headed to the control room, while I remained at the stern of the boat, waving and blowing kisses as Caleb navigated the ship to the boundary. As the figures on the beach grew tiny, I joined my husband. I took a seat by his side and looked at him.

His eyes were fixed forward in concentration. I followed his gaze, then spotted the hunters' gray ships surrounding our island.

"Do you think they'll detect us?" I asked.

"I don't know," Caleb replied. "But it doesn't matter too much. As long as none of them follow us."

"Yeah... That wouldn't make for such a relaxing trip."

Even though I knew we were safe within the witch's spell, my palms still grew sweaty as Caleb navigated the boat beyond the boundary. He moved slowly at first, skirting close to the boundary as he kept watch on the ships, and then he began speeding us away along the choppy waves, toward the wide-open waters.

Once we had traveled miles and the ships were nothing but dots in the distance, I was able to breathe more easily.

After two hours, Caleb was confident enough to put the boat on autopilot. He stood up and looked down at me, a small smile curving his lips. Taking my hand, he led me out of the control room and onto the moonlit deck. I breathed in the fresh salt air and looked around at the endless expanse of water, relishing the cool wind against my skin. The star-strewn sky was breathtaking. We walked to the front of the boat and stood listening to the rolling waves.

He stood behind me and his mouth found the back of my neck. He trailed kisses along my skin, which heated up beneath his touch. I bent my head backward so he could claim my lips. I felt his body tense against me. The next thing I knew, he was pulling me across the deck, down the staircase and into our bedroom. We took turns undressing each other, and then made love between the silk sheets.

Each time Caleb had slept with me since our wedding had been magic, but there was something about being on a boat again that made that night even more exhilarating. Our first time had been on a boat. That beautiful boat he had constructed for my birthday...

I'd been under the impression that the first time was always awkward, but it hadn't felt like that with Caleb. He'd taken me as he'd said he would. He'd made me feel owned, possessed, cherished, and he'd left no room for doubt or uncertainty.

Being so intimate with a vampire, I'd expected to feel more pain. But except for a dull ache between my thighs, I had barely felt discomfort. I wondered if my body was tougher than that of a regular human, or, perhaps more likely, the pleasure I found in Caleb's arms was too overpowering to feel much else.

Caleb often tensed up, and I could sense what a struggle it still was for him to reel in his craving for my blood. But he did. His fangs hadn't yet broken my skin. There were times, in the heat of his passion, when he seemed to forget his strength, but I was so used to

Caleb being gentle around me that, if I was honest with myself, I relished those moments of roughness and reveled in his abandon.

Hours passed, and by the time Caleb and I reached our climax again, morning had arrived.

I lay breathless against him, our legs still intertwined. He ran a broad hand down my back as his lips pressed against mine.

"You're on fire," he whispered, pulling me flush against his cool body.

"Now you know why I married you," I breathed back. "I needed a portable A/C unit."

His chest vibrated as he chuckled.

I imagined that had he been a human, I would be feeling far too hot to be so close to him right now. But Caleb being a vampire meant that there was rarely a time when I didn't cherish his embrace.

I blew out a sigh and nestled my head against his chest. Listening to the beating of his heart, I looked out of the tinted window at the sun's first rays reflecting in the waves.

The question that Claudia had asked me during her

and Yuri's welcome-home dinner played in my mind.

"Are you going to turn into a vampire, Rose?"

It was a question that had been at the back of my mind ever since Caleb had proposed to me. Of course, I'd always expected that I would turn as soon as my parents allowed it—but being married to a vampire made the issue more pressing.

There wasn't a day that went by when I didn't worry about Ben. None of us had any idea of when he would return. Or even if he would ever return. I couldn't lie to myself and pretend that question hadn't passed through my head, although I tried not to entertain the thought.

In the meantime, it was frustrating not knowing what was to become of my future. I didn't want to risk turning and becoming the same crazed bloodsucker my brother had woken up as. I couldn't become a risk to our people like he was.

And yet I felt that I had no choice but to turn into a vampire. My whole family were vampires now—except my father, although he would turn back into one soon. And most of my closest friends were supernaturals.

Even if Caleb was willing to turn into a human for me, which I knew he was, I just couldn't imagine living my life as a mortal and leaving everyone behind.

No. I had to turn into a vampire. And we had to find a way to solve my brother's problem, not run away from it.

I chewed on my lower lip.

"What's wrong?" Caleb asked, frowning as he looked down at me.

"What if I don't turn out like my brother?" I said.

"What do you mean?"

"What if Ben turned out the way he did not because of our blood? What if it's something unique to him?"

"You're twins. What makes you think that could be the case?"

"I'm not sure. I'm just thinking that all this time we've been assuming there is a danger of me turning out like him. But what if we're assuming wrong?"

Caleb remained staring at me, waiting for me to continue. Detaching myself from him, I rolled onto my back and gazed up at the ceiling. "When Ben and I were newborns, we got separated. He was taken to

Aviary… by none other than Kiev. I just wonder if the Hawks could've done something to him that even Kiev wasn't aware of. Or if the atmosphere affected him somehow. I already mentioned the idea to my parents, but of course, there is no way that we would know for certain… unless you tried turning me."

Caleb sat upright. I could see from the expression on his face that he didn't like where I was going with this. But I continued all the same. "If you tried turning me, one of two things would happen. I could turn out exactly like my brother, or I could turn into a normal vampire. If it was the former, we'd know for sure that there's something strange about our blood that causes this reaction, and we could eliminate the Aviary theory. But if I turned out all right… we'd be a step closer to understanding what's wrong with my brother, however small a step that might be."

"Why don't we save this talk of turning for when we return from our honeymoon? We'll have plenty of time to discuss this then with your parents and family."

I bit my lip. "The thing is… if we're going to try this, it would make sense to do it while we are away from The Shade, away from our humans, floating on a boat where you can control me…"

Caleb shot to his feet, wrapping a sheet around his waist. He stared down at me incredulously. "Is this supposed to be a joke?"

I shook my head.

He breathed out sharply. "What if you turned out exactly like him? Then what?"

"Then we'd have the opportunity to experiment on me, and figure out how to make me normal."

He looked at me in disbelief. "Rose, this is supposed to be a honeymoon. Honeymoon. Do you know what that word means? I'll tell you what it doesn't mean. A crazy, dangerous experiment in which neither of us understand what the hell we are doing and which could end up with you turning into a rampaging bloodsucker for all eternity."

Despite the seriousness of the subject, I couldn't help but find amusement in Caleb's exasperation.

"If things got really, really bad," I said, "we could return to The Shade and I could just take the cure."

Caleb scoffed. "'Just take the cure.' You speak of it

like it's popping a pill. You have no idea how painful it is."

"I do have an idea. My parents told me how much it hurts." I got up from the bed and walked over to him. Reaching for his hands, I held them gently and stopped him pacing.

He looked down at me, concern filling his eyes. "But just like turning into a vampire," he said, "it doesn't matter how much people have told you about the experience. There's no way to prepare for the agony."

"Maybe, Caleb," I replied softly. "But please understand… I need to try this, for my brother's sake and mine." I reached up to kiss his jawline. "And for our peace of mind."

He wet his lower lip. "And what about our children?" he asked, his brown eyes boring into mine. "Say for the sake of argument the turning did go fine, then what? If we want children, I would have to become a human in a few years anyway. What's the point in your becoming a vampire now when you would have to turn back soon? You'd be putting yourself through an unnecessary amount of pain—and risk."

"Because I don't want to wait that long. I'm fed up with living in uncertainty about our future and about my brother. I just want to at least do what's within our power to try to understand the situation."

Caleb turned his back on me and faced the window, leaning an arm against the frame. I remained in my spot a few feet away from him and didn't say a word. I needed to let him think.

When he finally turned back around to face me, I was relieved to see a look of resolve in his eyes.

"I understand what this means to you, Rose. I understand how hard it must be for you to have your twin go through what he has and to be living in such uncertainty. But it comes down to this: I'm not willing to inflict unbearable torture on my new bride during her honeymoon." He paused, a spark of sarcasm in his eyes. "Call me old-fashioned…"

"Then do it right at the end," I shot back, "just before we return."

He narrowed his eyes on me.

"That way," I continued, "we can enjoy a long,

peaceful honeymoon with no hurry to return. You can turn me when we come back, just a few miles from The Shade. So if things get really bad, you can take me back there quickly."

He still looked wary, but apparently he was struggling to find an argument against this compromise.

I walked up to him again, wrapping my arms around his waist and pressing my bare form against him. I kissed his chest, letting my tongue graze his skin. "Please, baby," I whispered.

He looked down at me, until finally he muttered:

"Your father is going to skewer me."

CHAPTER 9: DEREK

I stood in the Armory with Xavier and Ibrahim, eyeing the walls covered with weapons. Some had been newly developed by the witches, while others were as old as The Shade itself. I still remembered some of the stakes from the Battle of First Blood. They had aged well.

While each of us moved about and picked up a weapon every now and then, my thoughts drifted to my twins.

Although I hated the idea of both of them being away from The Shade at the same time once again, of course I couldn't deny Rose her honeymoon. She and Caleb more than deserved it. They had been through so much recently…

"Do we have enough?" Xavier asked, bringing me back to reality.

I eyed the weapons in each of our hands. "Yes," I said. "We're done here."

I left the Armory with the two men and stepped out onto the training grounds outside.

Although we had witches protecting us from the hunters, I couldn't help but feel uneasy at the fact that they were still watching us. If I knew exactly what their intentions were, it wouldn't be so bad, but not knowing… It was eating away at my nerves. It went against my every instinct as a ruler to just shut my eyes to them, even though our barrier was impenetrable to them.

So I had to change that. And there was only one way. Sofia was nervous about what I had planned, but she understood why I needed to do it and didn't bother attempting to persuade me otherwise.

We assembled all the weapons on the ground that

were suitable for use against hunters, and I picked three of the most deadly ones—guns—and holstered them at my belt.

Then I turned to Ibrahim. "Let's go."

Xavier slapped me on the back. "Good luck."

I nodded, and then touched the warlock's arm. Xavier and the rest of our surroundings vanished from sight and we reappeared at the end of the Port's jetty.

Ibrahim and I looked out toward the huge ships, still stationed in the exact same positions as they had been for days now.

"Which ship do you want to try first?" Ibrahim asked.

I didn't care much. I imagined that all of them would be similarly equipped. I pointed to the one furthest to our right.

"All right," Ibrahim said, and then clutched my shoulder. A second later, we had left the boundary of The Shade and emerged on the dark deck of the hunters' ship.

As I looked around the empty deck, the vessel appeared to be much larger than I had thought. Rows of chairs were positioned at the bow, directly facing The Shade, and they were surrounded by various telescopes and other spying equipment. This was where they sat and watched us.

Now, however, the deck appeared empty.

"Derek," Ibrahim muttered.

I could not see him because he had placed an invisibility spell over the two of us, but I felt him touch my arm, and the next thing I knew, he was tying a thin rope around my wrist. We had to stay connected. He was my ticket back to the island, and I couldn't afford to lose him.

Xavier had wanted to accompany Ibrahim and me, but of course, coming here with a bloodsucker was the most stupid thing we could do.

We remained in one spot for the next minute, continuing to look around, and then we moved toward the edge of the deck. Placing my hands over the railing, I looked downward. There were two rows of windows beneath us, one above the other.

Gripping Ibrahim's shoulder, I leaned in close to his ear. "Hover us down there so we can see through the windows," I said, in a voice barely louder than a breath.

I felt myself being lifted from the ground as Ibrahim levitated us until we were level with the first window. When we peered through it, it was clear that this was a cabin room. It was small, and there were two bunk beds. One man was sitting at a small table, reading a book. He wore a black polo neck shirt and black pants. Since there was nothing of importance here, Ibrahim moved us to the next window. Yet another cabin room. We continued moving around the ship at the level that we were on, but all we found were more cabins.

"Let's go further down," I whispered.

Ibrahim lowered us down a level, and now we began to see things that looked more interesting. Behind the first window was some kind of meeting room. It was a large room, and there was a long glass-topped table running down the center, with high-backed wheeled chairs around the edges of it. There was a light cream carpet on the floor, and everything looked sleek and modern.

We moved on to the next window, and here we found some kind of control room. The walls were lined with desks upon which sat dozens of computers and other equipment I couldn't put a name to. From where we hovered, I could make out five men—also wearing all black like the others we had seen previously. They were eating around a small table in the center of the room and were caught up in conversation, though I couldn't hear a word they were saying from outside. Even when I pressed my ear up against the glass, I couldn't hear the slightest thing. This was one thing that I found odd—Xavier and other vampires had tried to listen in from a distance to make out any conversations happening on the ships, but they had been totally unable. They should have been able to make out at least some human voices from where they stood listening. Now I was beginning to believe that these hunters had deliberately soundproofed the boat— yet another thing about their presence here for me to feel disconcerted about.

"I want to get into this room," I whispered to Ibrahim. "But in order for me to look around, I'm going to need you to create a distraction."

Ibrahim paused. "A distraction… Okay. I'll think of

something. But this will mean being separated for a while."

"That's all right. Just make sure that I stay invisible. I will stay in this room until you return. Say something when you enter so we can find each other."

Ibrahim grunted, and then he held my arm again. A moment later, we appeared inside the room. We emerged in one corner, and I remained deathly still, barely daring to breathe as the rope attaching the warlock to me slipped from my wrist and I felt the warlock's presence leave me alone with the hunters.

I backed up further against the wall as I watched the men cautiously. I was now able to hear what they were saying.

"How is Sarah?" one of them asked.

"Due in three months," another replied.

"Do you know what it's going to be?"

"We want it to be a surprise… How is your other half?"

The man sighed. "Jenny hasn't been well recently. She's been in the hospital more than she has been at home recently. But when I left, she was doing okay."

To my disappointment, the conversation continued in the same mundane vein, so I focused my attention on the computer monitors. I did not dare budge from my spot just yet, in case the floor creaked beneath me. So I remained standing as I was. I had to wait for Ibrahim to figure out a way to draw these hunters out of the room so I could explore.

Barely a minute later, a deafening siren went off. It was so loud, it reverberated around the entire ship. I had no idea what he had done—perhaps set off a fire alarm. In any case, his idea worked. The five men exchanged confused glances and, dropping their food, they ran out of the room.

As soon as all of them had exited, I walked over to the first monitor. The screen was blank, but I had learned a bit about computers from Sofia—at least, how to work a basic laptop. While these were certainly more complicated, I recognized that most of them appeared to be in sleep mode. The screens were dulled, but not completely black—there was still a light behind them. I moved the mouse. Nothing happened. I pushed a button on the keyboard. A pop-up appeared requesting a password.

Hm.

Moving away from that particular monitor, I scanned the rest of the computers. All of their screens were blank… except for one, in the far corner of the room. This was a taller and wider monitor than all the others. I walked up to it and stared at the computer, trying to make out what I was looking at. Possibly more than a thousand small white dots were speckled about the screen over a dark red background, and each moved around seemingly randomly. Some whizzed left and right, others moved slowly, while some weren't moving at all.

I scanned all corners of the monitor, looking for clues as to what this was. But it was in full-screen mode, so I saw nothing but the dots and red background. Placing a hand over the mouse, I moved it until a cursor showed on the screen. I glided it upward and clicked the minimize button.

A pop-up window appeared.

"Minimizing window will stall motion sensors. Hit 'Y' to continue, or 'N' cancel."

I held my breath as I stared at the words.

Stall motion sensors.

Realization fell upon me like a block of wood.

These white dots. They were my family. My friends. My people.

I didn't know how they were detecting our movements and keeping tabs on every single one of us. I could only guess that they must have some sort of advanced satellite technology that was able to sense movement that the witches' spell wasn't blocking.

A chill settled in at the base of my spine as I wondered what else they had discovered about us. How else they were watching us.

I started as Ibrahim's voice rose above the loud siren behind me. "Derek."

"What?"

"We need to go."

Before I could object, the warlock's hand closed around my shoulder and the next thing I knew, I was hurtling through air at the speed of light. When my feet hit solid ground again, we were back at the jetty of our Port.

My mind was reeling as I tried to process what I had

just witnessed. I felt irritated that Ibrahim had removed us from the ship after so little time. If I'd stayed longer, there were many more things that I might have discovered from that unlocked computer.

As he removed the invisibility spell from both of us, I turned on him.

"What happened?" I asked, trying to reel in my frustration. Ibrahim would not have brought us back here so soon without good reason.

He gazed back out at the ship we had just left, disturbance in his eyes.

"That alarm," he said, "I didn't set it off."

"What do you mean?"

"I mean I didn't deliberately set it off. I was vanishing myself from room to room, looking for a fire alarm of some sort to trigger, but as I paused in a corridor, that siren went off, and I... I heard someone yelling: 'Witch on board!'"

I stared at Ibrahim.

"Witch on board?" I repeated, wondering if I had somehow misheard.

He nodded, fixing his eyes on me. "The hunters are

gaining intelligence faster than we've given them credit for. They have sensors, a radar, or *something* on the ship that is incredibly astute." He looked like he was still in disbelief himself. "They were able to pinpoint not only that some kind of supernatural had set foot on the ship, but exactly what kind... I guess they didn't sense you because you're still a human. Perhaps they're not yet at the level of detecting a fire-wielder."

I held up a hand. "Wait. Are you sure that nobody could've seen you?"

Ibrahim breathed out impatiently. "No. I was invisible, Derek. Just as you were."

My mind reeled at the implications of Ibrahim's words. If they could detect witches, what other supernatural creatures could they detect? Vampires for sure, but what else?

And how on earth could they have developed such technology so quickly?

I had no idea how such systems could work. But I didn't need to understand. The fact was, the hunters were upping their game in ways that none of us—not even Eli or Aiden—had dreamed of. And now we knew for certain that it wasn't just vampires they were targeting, it was all supernaturals.

Although in theory Ibrahim and I could have stayed on the ship longer—after all, he was a powerful warlock—he'd been right to return us to The Shade. We did not know what tricks and surprises the hunters had up their sleeves with their new technology, and it was better not to aggravate them.

"Did you manage to discover anything at all?" Ibrahim asked.

After I explained what I had seen, his jaw dropped.

I looked up at the dark sky. "You and Corrine need to work on reinforcing the spell so that our movements will be invisible to their sensors also."

He nodded. "I'll go and see her. We'll try to fix this as soon as possible."

Then he vanished.

Casting one last glance back at the ships, I left the Port. As I made my way toward the Residences to find my wife, it chilled me to imagine those black-clad hunters watching my every step from their control room.

CHAPTER 10: SOFIA

I could hardly believe Derek when he told me what he and Ibrahim had discovered on their short trip to one of the hunters' ships. Although we didn't want to worry any of our people unnecessarily, we also didn't want to keep them in the dark, so we leaked the story about what Derek and Ibrahim had witnessed, and news soon spread to everyone.

Ibrahim and Corrine thought that they'd figured out how to tweak the spell so that the hunters could no longer sense our movements, and Mona helped them, although she had lost many of her powers when Lilith died.

There was outrage from the dragons when they found out that the hunters were watching us so closely. It seemed that some of them had not even been aware of the ships stationed around the island to begin with. Clearly they were very territorial creatures and Jeriad was immediately up in arms and wanted to go scorch the ships.

Of course, they could have done that, but that was not what Derek wanted, and that was not what I wanted either. We didn't want to cause more bloodshed or make enemies out of the hunters. So far at least, they had not harmed us—although we all knew what their intentions were. Still, we had no desire to spark a war between The Shade and the human world. We were on their side, even if they refused to believe it.

I was tempted to go with Derek to visit them and start a dialogue with the hunters, try to reassure them that we meant no harm, but my father said we would be crazy to do it. At this stage, he didn't think that they would even give us a chance to talk. He suspected that they might agree to meet with us but only as a trap and as soon as we were within range, we would be shot. And so that idea was pushed aside.

Derek forbade anyone to go outside of the boundary except with our express permission. He and I started going for walks along the beach every evening, to check if the ships were still there. Each time, they were. Weeks passed, and they still remained, just waiting and watching… for what exactly, we still weren't sure.

Although Derek was firm in his decision to let them be and not launch an attack, I could see the effect that the hunters' presence was having on him psychologically. I knew my husband, every part of him—often better than he knew himself. Even when we were talking about something else, I could sense it playing at the back of his mind, and I couldn't miss the worry behind his eyes.

Then one evening during our walk, to my dismay, we spotted two more large gray ships moored near the other three. My hand tightened around Derek's.

His brows furrowed as he stared out toward the new

vessels.

I was proud of him for how he'd handled the situation so far—it was quite unlike Derek. Usually he was not the first to suggest a peaceful course of action. Now I worried that if any more ships arrived, he might forget all notions of peace and just start planning to blast them out of the water. But this would not be good for anyone in the long term. And we had both witnessed too much bloodshed already.

But as I stood there with him that night, watching the dark outlines of the five ships above the waters, I wasn't sure what to say to him. I did not want to tempt fate and assume that he was going to resort to violence. So I just kept quiet and waited for him to reveal his mind to me.

But he didn't. He stayed just as silent as me. After ten minutes had passed, I didn't see the point in remaining out here longer. So we had five ships watching us now instead of three. It was what it was.

Turning to face him fully, I reached my arms up and draped them around his neck. I pulled his head down so that he was looking at me instead of the ships.

"Baby," I said softly. "Let's go to bed. You've had such a long day. Worry about it more in the morning, if you have to."

He looked reluctantly back at the ships, and then down at me. An expression of regret settled in on his handsome face. Dipping down toward me, he kissed my lips tenderly and whispered, "I'm sorry, Sofia. I haven't been present with you recently." He paused, brushing my cheek with his thumb. "But I promise I'll be yours tonight. All yours."

The smile that spread across his lips warmed me. He reached around me and picked me up. Relieved, I heaved a sigh and rested my head against his chest as he carried me back toward the forest.

I cast one last glance toward the ships. As Derek sped up, I was about to look forward again when I spotted something odd just beyond the boundary.

"Wait," I said.

Derek stopped, looking down at me in surprise. "What?"

He put me down on the sand so I could stand on my own two feet and then, grabbing his hand, I ran toward the water again. Just beyond the boundary, a smooth rounded surface stuck out from above the waves. It looked like… the roof of a submarine.

My heartbeat quickened.

"What is it, Sofia?"

I'd forgotten that Derek's eyesight wasn't as good as mine. "It looks like a submarine is trying to enter The Shade."

Derek cursed beneath his breath. "So they're actually trying to enter the island now…"

I moved into the waves until the water reached my waist. Something clicked, and a hatch opened. A head pushed out. The head of a man. I frowned in confusion as the rest of him was revealed and he stood up straight on the roof, his back facing us as he gained balance. He didn't appear to be armed with any weapons at all, and he wore just a loose checkered shirt and jeans. The way he was dressed… he did not look like a hunter. When he turned slowly to face us, I used my acute eyesight to study his face closely.

And then I gasped.

"What is it?" Derek said, his voice a mixture of

nervousness and impatience.

Vampire vision or not, I still wasn't willing to believe my eyes until I was standing right next to that man.

"To the Port!" I said.

Grabbing Derek's hand, I raced with him to the jetty and jumped into one of the submarines we had floating there.

"Navigate us toward that submarine," I said.

"Sofia, what the—"

"You'll see," I said breathlessly. "Just get us there quickly!"

He gave up trying to get an answer out of me and just hurried us forward as fast as the vessel would go.

I could see the belly of the submarine beyond the boundary as we approached. It was a small one, and it was… oddly familiar. My heart pounded as we arrived right next to it. I left the control room and climbed out of the hatch. In the time that it'd taken us to travel here, another person had climbed out of the submarine—now there were two humans standing on top of its roof.

A man and a woman.

Almost twenty years older than when I had last seen them.

Cameron and Liana Hendry.

CHAPTER 11: SOFIA

My voice caught in my throat, as did Derek's when he climbed up through our submarine's hatch and stood behind me.

"Cameron!" Derek gasped, his voice hoarse.

The redheaded man swiveled in our direction and looked around blindly.

"Derek?" he whispered, squinting. "Is that you?"

My heart leapt to hear his voice for the first time in so long. Cam's Scottish accent was still as thick as ever.

Without warning, Derek dove into the ocean and

resurfaced on the other side of the boundary. He gazed up at his two old friends whom he had shared centuries of his life with.

I leapt into the water too and swam until I bobbed in the waves next to Derek.

Cameron broke out into raucous laughter while Liana squealed at the sight of the two of us. The lines in Liana and Cameron's aged faces showed as they beamed. The couple bent down and stretched out their hands to us—but Derek and I could manage without their help. If anything, we might cause them to slip and fall into the water.

We climbed up next to them. Liana pulled me in for a tight embrace while Cameron enveloped Derek in a strong hug.

When we drew apart, all four of us just stared at each other, speechless.

"What are you, King Derek?" Cameron asked, half grinning and half frowning. "You're warm like a human, and yet you hardly look a day older than when we last saw you."

"And Sofia?" Liana said. "You're a vampire? I

thought you both turned back into humans."

Derek looked like he wanted nothing more than to just stand there and talk, as did I, but the two of us looked anxiously toward the direction of the hunters' ships.

"It's not safe out here," Derek said, clutching Cameron's shoulder. "Let's get on the other side of the boundary first."

"I guess it's been so long since we were last here," Cameron said, his voice reminiscent, "we don't have permission to enter The Shade like we used to."

"So many things have happened since you left, Cam," Derek said. "So. Many. Things. The spell has had to be recast a number of times."

We moved toward the hatch of their submarine, and the four of us slipped down into it and made our way toward the control room. I was surprised to see, sitting in two of the chairs behind the main switchboard, a young man and woman. They were in their teens, but they looked younger than Rose and Ben.

"Meet Cedric and Pippa," Liana said proudly.

The girl and boy stood up and shook our hands.

Pippa had blazing red hair, like her father, but she shared Liana's light amber eyes. Cedric on the other hand had dark blond hair, with Cameron's brown eyes.

I stared at the teens in confusion. When Liana and Cameron had left The Shade, they'd said that they wanted to trace their descendants. They'd lived centuries regretting having to leave their young children when they were first turned into vampires. Then when finally we'd discovered a cure, they'd wanted to leave The Shade to live a normal life and watch over some of their distant relatives. I wondered if perhaps these teens were such distant relatives.

"And who are Cedric and Pippa exactly?" I asked.

Cameron and Liana exchanged glances. "Our son and daughter."

I was speechless. I certainly hadn't expected them to have more children. But now that I thought about it, it made total sense. Hundreds of years had passed since they'd last lived as humans. The relatives who would still be living would be very distant indeed. They had still been young when they left, in their late twenties. I should've expected that they would start a new family.

"Wow," I said. Derek shared the same shocked expression as me.

I looked back at their two children. "What a pleasure to meet you. How old are you?"

"Fifteen," Pippa replied.

"I'm sixteen," Cedric said.

Apparently recovering from the shock, Derek proceeded to step behind the controls. "We should get inside."

He moved the vessel the few feet that it took to pass through the boundary, and then stopped. He turned to me. "We still have our submarine floating nearby. We have to take that back to the shore, so Sofia, you stay with Cam and Liana, and I will navigate the other submarine back. We'll meet at the Port."

Derek didn't look like he wanted to leave his two friends for even a minute after just reuniting with them, but we couldn't leave our submarine stranded.

And so he left, leaving me still reeling as I looked from Cameron, to Liana, to their two children.

"So how are you a vampire?" Liana pressed, clutching my knee as Cameron took a seat behind the controls and navigated the submarine toward the shore.

I breathed out, and traced my memory back to when they had first left The Shade. Rose and Ben had still been newborns, and Derek and I had also left The Shade to move into our dream home in California.

I didn't get far into our story before we arrived at the Port and Derek rejoined us.

We stepped out onto the jetty, and warmth filled Liana and Cameron's expressions as they eyed their old home.

"I've got to say," Cameron said hoarsely, "I've bloody missed this place."

I saw tears in the corners of Liana's eyes. She seemed quite choked up as she helped Pippa and Cedric onto the jetty next to them.

"You have no idea how excited everyone is going to be to see you again," I said, my heart pounding at the thought of Vivienne's eyes lighting up on seeing them again. Liana was her best and oldest friend. "We wondered what happened to you."

It was late now and most people were in bed, so as we led the four of them through the woods, the only person we bumped into was Eli taking Shadow for a nighttime walk. He looked like he had just seen a ghost as he eyed Liana and Cameron. Then a huge grin split his face and he hurried forward to embrace them.

Eli ended up joining us back in our penthouse after he had taken Shadow back to his apartment, and we spent the rest of the night trying to recount everything that had happened since they left.

I sat them down in the living room and since they all admitted that they were hungry, I prepared a meal for them of hot tomato soup with fresh bread, paella with feta cheese salad, and apple pie with ice cream, while we talked.

I kept looking at Cedric and Pippa. I wasn't sure how much their parents had told them of the supernatural world, and they looked in a daze listening to what we said. Heck, even Cameron and Liana looked in a daze—especially when we told them about our new fire-breathing residents.

Of course, there was no way to tell them everything that had happened in a matter of hours, but we did our best to provide a good recap.

And then it was our turn to ask questions.

"How come you never came to visit us all these years?" Derek asked. "And why are you here now?"

"Good questions," Cameron said, leaning back in his chair and taking a sip from his cup of tea. He glanced warmly at Liana. "My love and I... you know how we yearned for a normal life, Derek. Just as you and Sofia did. We wanted to experience what it was like to be human again. To live oblivious to the supernatural world. When we decided to have children, we knew we wanted to give them a normal, carefree upbringing. I guess if we hadn't had them, we probably would've come back to visit much sooner, but we wanted to shelter them. So once they were born, that just cemented our distance from The Shade. Actually, we only told them about... all this... about ten days ago."

My eyes widened. "Ten days ago?" *No wonder the poor kids look bewildered.*

Cameron paused, wetting his lower lip. "Something rather... disturbing happened. Something that left us no choice but to tell them the truth about our past, and return to The Shade."

Derek leaned forward in his seat. "What happened?"

"Two strange men showed up at our home in Scotland," Liana answered. "We were away on vacation at the time, in France. It was our house sitter who opened the door. They arrived late at night, around 9pm, and they asked to speak to Cameron and me. Our house sitter was under the impression that they were the police, so she gave them our mobile number. We received a call while we were on the beach one morning. It was an American man. It was Cameron who picked up the phone." She looked at her husband, who nodded.

"Yes, it was me," Cameron said. "He addressed me by my first and last name. He explained that he was part of a team working with the government to dig into some of the supernatural incidents that had been going on recently. The long and short of it was, he was a hunter and he knew who we were. I have no idea how he found out about Liana and me, and how he tracked us down, but he knew that we were once residents of The Shade. He said that we would be required to meet with them and this would not be a matter of choice. He asked how long we would be on vacation, so I told him the truth—we were due to return in a week." Cameron paused to eye his two children, who were watching him recount the story. "During that phone call," he continued, "we set up a time to meet, the very day after we returned, at noon. A couple of people would come to our house and ask us questions, or so they said. Well, we didn't wait that long. After I told Liana what had happened, we booked last-minute tickets and traveled back to Scotland the very same day. Reaching home in the middle of the night, we packed up in a frenzy, and thanked God that we had kept the sub in good condition all those years. We left within one hour—we dared not stay longer than that—and brought only the possessions that we really needed."

I stared at the couple, my mouth open. I couldn't imagine how traumatic that must've been, to leave what had likely been twenty years' worth of memories within the space of an hour, never to return again. Especially for their son and daughter.

Derek also looked taken aback. "So you left...just

like that."

Cameron raised a brow. "Of course, Derek. It was obvious that the only reason they wanted to meet with us was to get intelligence on The Shade. And who knows what means they would have resorted to in order to force the information out of us. Leaving was our only option. We could never betray you."

"Besides," Liana said, "it was about time that we returned to visit you."

"This isn't a visit though, is it?" I said. "You're here for good now."

Cameron and Liana nodded slowly.

I looked at their children for a reaction. They both appeared to be surprisingly resolved about the idea. Of course, we had plenty of youths here they could make friends with. It would just be a shock getting used to life on this strange dark island.

"There are five hunter ships outside the boundary now, watching the island," Eli said, looking seriously at Cameron through his spectacles.

"But so far that's all they've done," I said. "Watch."

A silence fell as Cameron and Liana looked at us

uneasily.

"You haven't considered launching an attack to get rid of them?" Cameron asked.

Derek glanced my way. There was an undercurrent of conflict in his expression, but I was relieved when he replied, "For now they have done nothing to directly harm us. And in the long term, The Shade clashing with the human world will not be good for anyone. We need to avoid bloodshed as much as possible."

A small smile curved Cameron's lips. "You've changed your tune, Novak. Since when are you a pacifist?"

Derek clenched his jaw, eyeing me once again. "Believe me, Cameron, this tune is grating at my nerves every second of the day."

CHAPTER 12: RIVER

After the day the blood rain fell, the echoing in Ben's and my ears became more frequent.

Ben said that he heard not only sounds of the atrium, but a voice too—an eerie chant that played over in his mind. I was bewildered as to how it could've known his name—whatever "it" was.

Ben was more determined than ever to reach The Shade. He maintained that there were witches there more knowledgeable and experienced about all things supernatural than he was, and that they might be able to offer insight as to what was happening to us. As soon as we arrived, he said, I would enter The Shade to try to figure out not only whether I could turn back, but also what had happened to us in The Oasis that was causing this torment.

Although the sounds of that desert prison surrounded us instead of the calming waves, as days passed, we didn't have another incident like the blood rain. In fact, as we sailed through the Red Sea, the journey began to take on an almost lethargic pace. Even despite the echoing in our ears, we started to find a semblance of peace in each other's company—or at least I did in Ben's.

Although it had been terrifying, it turned out that the shower of blood had been a mercy for Ben. When the blood fell upon us from the heavens, most of it had escaped as it streamed across the deck, but there had been three empty barrels that had filled almost halfway. As soon as Ben noticed them, he took them down to the small storage room beneath the deck which was the coolest room on the boat. Of course, without any way to treat it, the blood wouldn't take long to congeal. But

I guessed that he'd find a way to consume it and at least wouldn't starve. I wasn't sure what happened to vampires without blood. Whether they could even starve. I was glad I didn't need to find out.

Thinking about what I would do if something happened to Ben made me realize just how dependent I was on him. Without him, I would perish. I'd no idea how to navigate the boat, and much less of an idea of how to live in this world as a supernatural. And being dependent was something I hated. Since my father left, I'd tried to become as self-reliant as I could.

Of course, Ben was just as dependent on me. Heck, he might've gone through the whole of Cairo slaughtering people if I hadn't been there to help him regain control in that guesthouse office.

It was ironic. Despite Ben's uncontrollable thirst for blood, I realized as the days passed that he was actually an easy person to get along with—at least I found him so. We both worked together to figure out practical day-to-day things, like having clean clothes to wear. Since I had only one pair of clothes, as did he, which were already dirty from our trip even before we left

Ismailia, we ended up fashioning clothes for ourselves out of spare bed sheets—clothes being a very generous term. I just cut one to size and tied it around my chest so that it hung like a strapless dress, while Ben wore one around his waist.

As for food for myself, I was lucky that there was a stash of it in the storage compartment—all of it longlife food in packets and tins, and none of it tasty, but it was keeping me full.

Since there was only one bed in the bedroom, and not really enough room for one of us to sleep on the floor, I ended up sleeping alone at night. There was a couch up on the deck, and that was where Ben took naps when he felt like it—although he really didn't sleep much. It was hard for me to sleep in the beginning. I wasn't used to resting alone, nor was I used to the rocking motion of the boat, but after a week or so, I'd gotten used to it.

At night, we got into the habit of lighting up a small fire on the deck, inside a wide metal container that we found out in the storage room. It was during those nights that I began to enjoy getting to know Ben better. Not just as the vampire, but as the human he'd been before he'd turned, and the human he still was when his bloodlust was at bay.

Finally one night, as we sat next to each other, I plucked up the courage to ask him the question that I had found myself wondering more and more recently.

"Do you have a girlfriend?"

He gave me a smile. "Why?"

I felt blood rush to my cheeks a bit. I'd been hoping that he wouldn't ask me that. "Just curious."

"No, I don't," he replied. "Do you have a boyfriend?"

I shook my head. I'd had crushes in high school before, but never a boyfriend.

I looked away from his face and down at the fire. Though I could feel his gaze still on me. I busied myself with my mug of instant hot chocolate, blowing on the liquid and tracing the rim of the cup with my finger.

"Well, I quite like you, Benjamin," I said. "Especially when you're not acting like a serial killer."

He chuckled. "I like you too, River. This situation…

sucks. But I'm honestly grateful that it's you that I ended up stranded with."

I raised a brow, prompting him to clarify.

He leaned back, resting on his palms as he looked at me, a thoughtful expression on his face. "You make me feel…" He paused. "Like I'm not Satan."

I snorted. "Well, thank you."

"You should take that as a compliment," he said, a wry smile forming on his lips. "Not even my family could manage it."

Setting my mug down, I bowed my head in honor. "Do you think they might present me with some kind of reward for being the one to tame the prince?"

"What kind of reward would satisfy you?"

Good question, I thought as I looked into his vivid green eyes. Eyes I was beginning to lose myself in.

"I… I, uh…" I found myself tongue-tied.

I knew what I should say—that all I wanted was to turn back into a human so I could return to my family—yet somehow, that wasn't what I felt like saying in this moment as we sat together. I bit my lower lip.

Then something made me lean closer to him, and rest my head against his shoulder.

His arm slid around me.

I leaned up to kiss his cheek, then looked back at the fire. His fingers played with the tips of my hair, tugging gently against my scalp. It felt like a kind of massage, and, combined with the warmth of the fire, made me feel deeply relaxed.

Then his palm brushed over my forehead, moving aside my hair, and his lips pressed against the top of my head. Tingles ran down my spine and when he stopped, I found myself wishing his kiss had lasted longer.

My thoughts were interrupted as the boat rocked violently.

Detaching himself from me, Ben shot to his feet.

"What was that?" I whispered.

He raised a finger to his lips.

I heard the clanging of metal. It came from the stern of the boat, which was out of view from where we'd been sitting. We crept toward the control room in the center of the boat and peered around it.

Four tall, thin African men were standing on the deck, carrying guns. I gasped.

At first I thought they might be hunters. But something about their appearance told me they were not. For one thing, their guns looked too outdated, and their clothes were ragged and tattered.

"Who are these men?" I breathed, as a fifth man clambered on board and they began to walk toward us in the shadows.

"Pirates," Ben whispered. "Wait here."

Pirates. Of course, it made sense. By now we had reached the Gulf of Aden. Looking closer at the men, it appeared that they were Somali pirates.

Oh, dear.

They really picked the wrong boat.

CHAPTER 13: RIVER

The pirates barely managed to release a gunshot before Ben sprang on them. Considering they might've even intended to kill us in order to hijack the boat, I couldn't bring myself to feel too much sympathy for them. Still, I couldn't bear to watch the scene. I'd witnessed too much gore already. I turned around and sat down by the fire, my hands over my ears as I tried to distract myself from what was going on at the stern of the ship.

After Ben had finished with them, he came into

view, splattered with blood. I assumed that he had killed all five of the men. I wouldn't have been surprised if he had drained all of them in one go. I didn't understand how he actually contained all that blood in his body. It was a mystery to me.

He had a look of satisfaction on his face, that much was undeniable, but he also looked guilt-ridden—just as he had looked during the attack in the guesthouse.

He stepped into the control room and, to my surprise, stopped the engine. Once the boat had slowed down, he stepped out and walked to the edge of the railing.

"What are you doing?" I asked.

"Going for a dip."

He removed the sheet around his waist, now just in his boxer shorts, and dove into the sea. I walked up to the railing and watched him submerge and then re-emerge, rubbing his face. Although it was a cool night, I decided to join him since I was feeling sticky myself.

Fastening my sheet dress so that it wouldn't slip off the moment I dropped in the water, I dove into the sea and resurfaced near Ben.

The water was rougher than I had expected. As I neared Ben, a wave carried me right up close to him—so close I ended up colliding with him. His hands caught my waist, the strength of his arms engulfing me as he kept me in place, anchoring me. I placed my arms around his neck as we floated together in the waves.

My eyes level with his, I gazed into his green irises that reflected the glimmer of moonlight on the waters.

His breathing became more uneven. His eyes fell to my lips.

Slowly, he reached a hand up into my hair at the back of my head. The next thing I knew, he was leaning in closer. And then his lips were on mine.

I breathed hard, pulling him closer as his mouth locked with mine. I tasted the salt on his lips, felt their coolness, their firmness as they pushed against mine and closed around them. When the tips of our tongues touched, fireworks erupted in my chest.

I had never kissed a boy before. But Ben's kiss was everything I had imagined it would be… and so much more.

Even the echoes in my ears that I'd heard again

earlier that evening vanished completely as I was consumed by the vampire prince of The Shade.

CHAPTER 14: JERAMIAH

I looked around the room at the sacks of ground human bones that Michael and I had just finished processing in the machine. We had done extra this week and there were too many to carry downstairs comfortably, so Lloyd came to assist us. Entering the prison beneath the atrium, we walked swiftly past the half-bloods' and humans' cells, traveling deeper and deeper into the maze of cells until we reached the farthest chamber that was hidden behind a storage room. Entering inside, I told Lloyd and Michael that they could leave.

Looking down at the trap door in the center of the room, I bent down and lifted it open to reveal a dark, metal chute. A fragrant aroma of cooking wafted out. *I'm just in time.* I dropped the sacks through one by one before closing the trapdoor.

If this were a usual day, my work in this room would be done now. But today, I had something else to accomplish.

Opposite the main entrance to the room was a smaller, narrower door. I pulled it open and began making my way down the staircase behind it. Reaching the bottom, I found myself standing in the corner of a kitchen the size of a large hall. Everything about it oozed extravagance, from the table tops made of solid gold to the shiny silver cutlery.

Several large pots were bubbling over stoves and snake heads were baking in the giant oven. The sacks of ground bones I had just dropped through the chute were piled up in a heap in one corner, ready for the chef to return.

Passing through the kitchen, I opened its rosewood

door and stepped out into another atrium. Situated directly beneath ours, this atrium was similar in design, except that it was much larger and immeasurably more luxurious. There was barely an inch of surface that wasn't made of some kind of precious stone or metal, and in the center was row upon row of celestial fountains. It was truly a glimpse of heaven.

I began to make my way along one of the heavily ornamented verandas when a veil of light blue mist appeared before me. I stopped and stared at it until the body of a man manifested in thin air from the waist up. Beneath his torso was nothing but the light blue mist, which had thickened and now looked more like smoke. With gleaming golden eyes, long, curling black hair and a thickset jaw, Karam levitated before me.

Karam Nasiri—brother of the head of the Nasiri family of jinn. Our cohabitants and self-proclaimed masters of The Oasis.

"I have brought you three times the requested amount of supplies today," I said. "Now my wish is to see your sister."

He frowned at me, then nodded. "All right," he

replied, his voice low and throaty. "Come with me."

He kept himself manifested so I could see him, and I followed him as he levitated toward the uppermost level of the jinn's atrium and stopped outside a gold-plated door studded with red rubies.

He opened it and moved inside. "Wait here," he said, before closing the door behind him.

I stepped back and leaned against the wall of the veranda, looking down at the sparkling fountains below.

Sometimes I still couldn't believe that we had lived this way all these years. When my coven and I had first escaped the Elders decades ago and I'd gotten the idea to come to The Oasis, we'd had no idea what we might find here. We'd guessed we'd come upon—at the most—a ruined palace. And indeed that was what we'd found. With the help of our five witches, we'd renovated and built up The Oasis into the beauty that it was today and placed a protective spell over it. What we hadn't realized was that The Oasis had already been inhabited since the Maslens had lived here. The place had been infested with a family of jinn—one of the oldest of this mortal realm.

We had already put so much effort building up this place and making it our home, when we discovered what we were living with, we couldn't find it in ourselves to move.

And yet the jinn, who had made their palace deep underground, would not allow us to live in peace without submitting to their rules—not even our witches could resist them. At the time, I didn't know where else we would go. We didn't want to risk leaving The Oasis to get stranded in the desert or be discovered by hunters, so we'd seen it as the lesser of two evils to stay, and provide them with certain… luxuries.

Some of our vampires had protested and refused to cooperate. They all ended up leaving, and we never saw them again. We didn't know what had happened to them—whether they'd escaped the desert safely or not. The rest of us who decided to stay were marked by the jinn, initiated as part of their extended family.

It certainly took some getting used to—I'd never seen a jinni in my life and hadn't even known they existed until arriving here. I'd hated everything about them at first—the way they used their wish-granting powers to manipulate a person's mind and always twisted things for their own benefit—and truth be told I still did. But as time had gone by, I had gotten used to them. If there was one thing I'd learned in all my dealings with the creatures, it was important to control one's mind and one's desires around them. They thrived on uncontrolled emotions and unfulfilled wishes. That was how they manipulated their victims. The more you desired in this place, the more sway they had over you, and the more indebted you became.

That said, they did treat us as family, in that they saw us as their own. So long as we remained loyal to them, we could count on their protection and help in times of need. They granted us wishes and luxuries to live how we wanted upstairs, and allowed as many half-bloods as we wanted—provided that we stuck to a fixed ratio of half-bloods to humans we collected. They never wanted us to overstep this ratio, since the humans were primarily caught for their bones, for the jinn. The blood we derived from them was just a byproduct, in the jinn's eyes, and they saw half-bloods as solely servants of the vampires. This ratio was an assertion of their superiority over us—something they always liked to remind us of.

"You may see me now." A silky female voice spoke behind me, breaking through my thoughts.

I turned around to find myself standing before the unearthly form of Nuriya Nasiri. Queen Nuri, as they called her. Like her brother, she too floated on a cloud of pale blue smoke, and only half of her stunning form was visible. Her ivory skin shimmered as she laid her golden eyes on me.

"Come in, Jeramiah."

I followed as she led me inside her lavish apartment. She showed me into her living room and I took a seat on one of the silk embroidered couches.

She remained levitating a few feet away. "What is your wish?"

"Tell me who Joseph Brunson really is."

CHAPTER 15: JERAMIAH

I had suspected for a while now that Joseph had lied about his identity, though I wasn't sure who he was exactly. It had been eating at me since the day I'd begun to suspect it and I knew I wouldn't be able to get it out of my mind until I got an answer. And so I'd decided to use up a hard-earned wish to find this out.

Nuriya eyed me. Then, moving to the center of the room, she pointed to the floor. It had been empty just a few seconds before, but now a swirling pool of mist hovered over it, and was beginning to form a scene.

Wide-open waters. A sea. Or an ocean. There was a black dot in the center of it, which was growing larger and larger as the vision zoomed closer. Soon it was clear enough to see a boat coming into view. And the two people on board. Joseph and his half-blood girl, River.

"So you want to know who this man is," she said calmly.

"Tell me."

"His name is Benjamin Novak."

My voice caught in my throat. I looked up from the swelling vision and stared at the jinni.

"Novak?" I stuttered, wondering if I had misheard.

"Novak," she repeated.

"Our surnames are not a coincidence? He is related to me?"

"You are cousins."

Cousins.

I stared back down at the vision, now scrutinizing every aspect of Joseph's—Benjamin's—appearance.

I'd never laid eyes on my father, not even in a photograph. So I had no idea what he'd looked like, nor what his younger brother and sister looked like. Nor any of the rest of my family for that matter. But now that I thought about it, I could see similarities in Ben's and my appearance.

"He is the prince of The Shade," Nuriya continued. "The son of Derek Novak, king of The Shade."

The Shade.

My breathing became heavier as the jinni's words sank in.

Benjamin was my cousin.

He was prince of The Shade, while his father was king.

I knew from the jinn that it was Benjamin's grandfather who had murdered my father. His whole family were my father's sworn enemies.

If it weren't for them, I would've been able to meet my father today. He would still be alive. Hell, after my grandfather, Gregor Novak, Lucas Novak had rightful rule over The Shade. He was the oldest of the three siblings.

If it weren't for Benjamin's family, I would be prince of The Shade right now, not living in this jinn-infested desert.

I was losing control of my emotions. I needed to calm down.

Regulating my breathing, I stilled my mind, forcing my thoughts away from the injustices and back to the present time.

"I see that I have upset you," Nuriya said softly.

Loosening my clenched fists, I cleared my throat and shook my head. "No. I am quite all right."

I looked again at the figures of River and Benjamin Novak—now swimming in the ocean near the boat.

"I just wonder," I said after a pause, "why have you not reclaimed them already?"

Nuriya smiled, revealing a set of pearly white teeth that were far too thick and strong for a human's.

"Sometimes loved ones need a little time before they realize what is good for them…" Her voice trailed off as she glanced at Benjamin and River once more before vanishing the swirling vision. "You know what I mean?"

I nodded.

"Jeramiah," Nuriya continued. "Benjamin Novak

and River Giovanni are two of our own now. Now that I have answered your question, you do not have permission to harm him. Do you understand?"

I smiled courteously.

"I wouldn't dream of it. I do, however, have one other request…"

CHAPTER 16: Ben

Staying with River on the boat for so many days, I was relieved when we finally kissed. I'd felt the tension building up between us, and I'd wanted to kiss her much sooner. I suspected that she had too. We just hadn't found the right moment.

With the guilt of claiming yet more human lives fresh in my heart and mind, River brought me the release of emotion I needed.

Closing my eyes as I continued to taste her lips, I pushed her up against the side of the boat. My hands roamed her body, exploring her curves through the thin sheet she wore in a way I hadn't had the chance to do until now.

I kissed her harder. Too hard. She let out a soft moan as my fangs caught her lower lip. I should've raised my head to see if she was all right, but the fact that her lips continued to knead passionately against mine a moment later told me that she was. I was so consumed by the sweetness of her kisses, I barely noticed the bitterness of her blood.

The current parted her sheet-dress. I tensed as I felt the bare skin of her upper thigh brush against my right hip. Something about that touch intensified my desire for her and before I knew what I was doing, I'd gathered her in my arms and leapt back onto the boat with her.

I didn't know what I was planning to do, or why I had just lifted her out of the water. My brain seemed to have shut down, my passions leading the way. All I knew was, the closer I felt to River, the more I touched and kissed her, the more the pain and darkness shrouding my mind diminished.

My feet carried us down into the depths of the boat, toward River's bedroom. But just before I stepped inside, I stopped short.

What am I doing?

I detached my lips from hers and set her down on her feet.

My eyes traveled the length of her, the wet sheet clinging to her soft curves.

She didn't know how alluring she was to me in that moment. How much I wanted her…

I swallowed hard.

It took all the willpower I had to step back.

She looked at me, wide-eyed and breathless. Her lips, flushed red, were slightly parted.

Although I wanted her, part of me was influenced by the need to forget that I'd just murdered again, and I knew that I would regret it if I took things any further with River tonight.

I cleared my throat, even as I continued to take in her beauty.

I found my voice again. "Good night, River."

"Good night," she replied, hoarsely.

I sensed hunger in her eyes, which made me believe that she felt the same heat.

But this wasn't right. Not now. And not like this.

***

We were both awkward around each other when we crossed paths in the corridor beneath deck the next morning. She looked up at me through her dark lashes, her expression bashful.

"I… uh, good morning," she murmured.

Every moment of last night played in my mind. Our kiss. What might have happened if I'd let it…

"I don't want things to feel awkward between us now," I said quietly.

My glance moved to her lips and I felt the urge to taste them again. Breaking the ice, I took a step closer to her, slid a hand beneath her chin and tilted her head upward. I lowered my head and brushed my lips against her neck, her cheek, before kissing her full on the mouth.

Her breath hitched, but then a smile spread across her face.

"Neither do I," she whispered, twining her fingers with mine and planting my hands on her waist. "But I'm glad we held back last night."

"I am, too," I said, relieved that she felt the same way.

It was clear that we both had too much on our minds, too many obstacles to overcome, to start a relationship in that way. But at least I'd feel more relaxed in her presence now that we were being honest about our attraction for one another.

"But," she continued in a low voice, draping her arms around my neck and drawing me down closer to her again, "I'd like you to keep kissing me."

I pulled her body flush against mine. The tips of our noses touching, I whispered:

"I'll see what I can do about that…"

***

Our journey across the Arabian Sea was thankfully uneventful. The echoes in our ears continued, but by now, this was no longer shocking. As we neared Sri

Lanka, it became clear to me that we would need another vessel. There were things going wrong with this one, and we'd almost come to the end of our supply of extra fuel.

We neared Colombo early afternoon, but we waited until evening before approaching the shore. I grabbed River's backpack, filled with cash and the coins that hadn't yet been converted, as well as the vial of amber liquid that she didn't want to let go of yet. I took her hand, and we abandoned the boat along a deserted beach and began to run toward the port. River had washed our robes in the sea and dried them on the deck in preparation for our arrival, so at least we weren't running around in bedsheets.

We soon arrived at the main harbor and our search for a new vessel began. River pointed out a few, suggesting that I check them out, but this time, I was looking for something different than just a regular boat. What I wanted was a submarine. But one proved to be hard to find. There weren't many around. And those I did spot were far too difficult to break into without damaging the vessel. But eventually, I found one in a private bay area that I managed to gain entry to.

There was terror in River's eyes as we lowered ourselves inside. I could practically see the image of another set of security guards chasing us in her imagination. Thankfully, this time we weren't chased—at least we didn't notice anyone. I was able to start up the submarine without much delay, since it was quite an outdated vessel, and then I navigated us away from the harbor. I glanced at River to see her staring at the control panel as she took a seat next to me.

"You're... really smart," she said, running a hand over the panel. "I wouldn't be able to start this thing if you gave me a million bucks."

"It helps when your uncle has been teaching you since you were a kid," I replied.

"Well, you have a cool uncle."

I smiled to myself. "Yeah. I guess my family is pretty cool."

River paused, wetting her lower lip. She fixed her gaze straight ahead through the windscreen at the dark waters rushing past.

Then she said, "If one of your witches manages to figure out how to cure me, how will I get back to New York?"

"That is going to be the least difficult part," I replied. "Our witches can transport you there by magic. I promise it will be the fastest journey you have ever been on."

"And… If I turn back, will I ever see you again?" Her voice sounded strained.

I wasn't sure how to answer that. "Once I've figured out what's wrong with me—assuming I manage to— and I return to The Shade, you could come visit me."

She shifted uncomfortably in her seat.

"Yeah," she said. "I guess so. But how would I contact you?"

Again, that was a difficult question. Neither my parents nor the witches liked to just give out phones to anyone. They didn't like lots of lines of communication open into The Shade, unless it was for emergency purposes. Still, I was sure that I could convince Corrine to give one to River.

"I would try to sort something out for you. We'll have your address also, so we know where to find you."

"Okay," she said, her voice now sounding dry and hoarse. "Because… Ben, I really like you."

Averting my gaze away from the controls again, I was surprised to see that she had tears moistening the corners of her eyes.

I put the vessel on autopilot temporarily and stood up, walking over to her and running my hands down her shoulders. I bent down to her level, brushing my lips against her cheek. "Hey, it's okay. We'll find a way to see each other."

She stood up, allowing me to gather her in my arms. She pressed the side of her face against my chest and took a deep breath, holding me tight.

"Thank you," she said. "I hope we can stay friends even if nothing more… at least, until I get too old for you."

I leaned down and caught her soft lips in mine, kissing them gently.

"You're getting a bit of ahead of yourself, you know," I said, attempting to bring out a smile in her.

"We don't even know if you can turn back into a human yet. You might be stuck as a half-blood whether you like it or not."

She gave me a weary smile.

I sat back down in my seat and, holding her hand still, pulled her down to sit on my lap. She crossed her legs over mine and draped her arms around my neck. We continued kissing before she raised her head and said, "When we were back in the desert, after Jeramiah let us go free... saying goodbye to you then... that was really hard."

I brushed my thumb against her cheek. "I know."

"I... I kind of wanted to kiss you then."

"You did kiss me."

"Yeah, on your cheek."

I paused, thinking back to the time we were within the atrium and I had told River to pretend that she was kissing me. I had gotten carried away myself. "Well I wanted to kiss you even before that. When we were pretending to make out."

The small amount of blood that she had in her cheeks rose to the surface, giving her face a cute pale pink glow. She smirked. "Yeah, that got me a bit hot and bothered."

We made out until I'd made her breathless again, and then she sat back down in her seat.

"Are there lots of people our age in The Shade?" she asked.

"Yes," I replied. "There are lots of people of all ages in The Shade. It's kind of a place for everyone."

"You must be the hottie of the island."

I rolled my eyes. It would be a lie to say that it wasn't a constant effort to keep girls at bay back home. But that wasn't something that I was interested in boasting about or letting on to. So I chose not to respond to her comment.

"And what about you, beautiful? I was surprised when you told me that you've never had a boyfriend. I would've thought that you'd be the target of all the boys in your class."

She shrugged. "I guess I don't make myself very approachable. And I've had family problems, lots of them. Even if I did get asked out, I'd never really have felt stable enough to commit myself much... You, um, you're the first boy I've ever kissed."

"Wow… I, uh, wouldn't have guessed if you hadn't told me. You're a great kisser."

She grinned.

I was glad that she had told me. Knowing that I had been her first was something that I didn't take lightly.

"You said that your brother is autistic," I said. "Is that the 'family problems' you're referring to?" I hoped that my question wasn't intrusive. I didn't want to pry into something that wasn't my business, but I felt genuinely curious.

"Well, my dad has been… kind of an asshole, shall we say. He's actually in jail right now. He's been sentenced to ten years."

"Oh. I'm sorry," I said.

"Nothing to be sorry about," she said. "It's just life… He put a real strain on our finances before he left, and my mom has been struggling for a while to care for all of us, including a disabled nineteen-year-old. So I got into the habit of working a lot to help out. My grandfather, he's comfortably wealthy, and has often offered money, but, well, he and my mom fell out recently and things have been awkward between them… Anyway. I don't want to bore you with my sob story."

I was silent for a few moments, thinking about her words.

"You're a strong person, River," I said.

She shrugged. "As my mom would say, when life throws stuff at you, you either duck or catch." She paused, then changed the subject. "You keep saying how you want to cure yourself of your human bloodlust, but do you have any idea how long that is going to take? Or how you're going to do it?"

If I was honest with myself, since I'd realized that River was my responsibility, and I had offered to bring her to The Shade, I had postponed thinking in depth about my problems almost entirely. My focus had been on fulfilling my promise to River and getting her to The Shade in one piece. Once her situation was sorted, I'd be able to direct my attention to my own problems.

"I'm not sure how to answer either of those questions yet," I replied.

She shifted in her seat. "I just… I feel like you've

helped me so much. Is there anything that I could do to help you?"

I looked at her seriously. "River, you have helped me—have no doubt about that. You've helped me more than you realize."

"It doesn't feel like it, at least not compared to what you have done for me."

"Well, I can't think of a way you could solve my problem permanently. I also don't know where my mystery might lead me, and I wouldn't want to drag you into any more danger than you've already been through."

She looked down at her feet, appearing dissatisfied by my answer. But she said, "Okay."

After that, we were mostly silent for the next few hours, apart from a bit of small talk.

Once I felt confident to leave the submarine on autopilot, I caught River's hand and led her toward the back of the submarine where we explored the rooms—something we hadn't had time for until now, due to being so bent on escaping the harbor at Colombo. It was much bigger than I had estimated. There were five cabins with single beds, three toilets, a galley, and a small sitting area. River said that she wanted to take a shower, so we parted ways in the corridor. I headed to one of the bedroom cabins and sat down on the single bed, leaning against the wall.

I wasn't sure what I was going to do for human blood now that we were in a submarine bound for the Pacific. I'd ended up finishing the blood that we had caught in barrels from the blood shower while we were still on the ship. So for now, I wasn't craving. But sooner or later, I would start feeling the thirst again.

That had been the advantage of being in The Oasis—at least there, I never had to worry about running out of human blood. It was restocked in my fridge as if by magic the moment I began running low. Now, I had to start thinking about possibly murdering another innocent person in the near future.

I wasn't sure how I was going to last all the way to The Shade, and then waiting for River, and then traveling back somewhere else, to wherever my next destination was. No. It was inevitable. Somehow, I would have to get human blood. Perhaps stop on a remote island and find some hospital where the patient was already dying. That was the most humane way I could think of to satisfy myself.

I brought myself back to the present. For now I was full, and I had River with me, who would hopefully stave off my cravings longer than usual.

By the time I was finished with my musings, I heard the bathroom door click next door, and River's footsteps as she stepped out of the shower.

There was a knock at my door, and then she stepped inside. Her long hair was wrapped up in a towel, and she was wearing her black robe again.

"I was thinking how Lalia wasn't marked with a tattoo," River said, taking a seat next to me on the bed as she unwrapped her hair and began drying it with the towel. "Neither was Hassan or Morgan. I wonder why?"

I shrugged. "Perhaps because they'd been intended solely for, uh, consumption."

River shuddered. "Thank God we got them out of there." Parting her hair into three bunches, she began working it into a braid. "I also keep thinking about that vial in my bag. I-I just can't shake the feeling that it's something to help my brother. That dream I told you about, where I imagine having a normal conversation with him, it keeps coming back."

"Maybe," I said, "but would you really risk giving it to him? What if it was something else?"

She looked nervous at the thought. "Yeah, that's what I've been—"

The submarine jolted, sending River flying off the bed. Before I could catch her, she'd slammed against the wall. She cursed, rubbing her head. I would've gone flying too had I not gripped hold of the bed to stop myself from crashing into her.

As the submarine steadied, I crouched next to her and examined her head. "Are you okay?"

"I'll survive," she grumbled.

I hurried out into the corridor and entered the control room. I stared through the window at the murky waters, trying to get a clue as to what had just happened. Something had obviously collided with us. But what? It must've been some kind of large creature—a shark, possibly even a whale. River joined me a few moments later and the two of us scanned the waters.

My heart leapt into my throat and River let out a scream as a creature shot up from beneath the submarine. A creature unlike anything I'd seen in my life.

She appeared to be a woman, with scaly green skin and matted purple hair that covered her bare chest. Her hideous face was pressed right up against the glass, her thin lips parting to reveal fangs. She slid upward against the screen, glaring down at us through yellow eyes. She moved higher and her bottom half came into view—the tail of a fish.

My God. Is this a…

River finished my sentence for me, her voice choked with horror. "A mermaid?"

She screamed again as the creature brought a fist down against the reinforced glass. She slammed against it so forcefully, I felt the floor beneath me tremor. If she continued to hit like that, I didn't know how much longer the glass would hold up.

I moved closer to her, baring my fangs and giving

her a menacing look, hoping to scare her back.

It didn't. If anything, it only aggravated her. Now she began bringing both fists down at the same time. I could hear her snarling through the water.

Dropping into the control seat, I ramped up the speed of the submarine suddenly, tilting downward, then upward, sideways right and left, hoping to jerk her off the vessel. But she remained clinging as though her hands had suckers on them.

There was a thud against the roof of the submarine. A few seconds later, another equally hideous creature slid down the screen, taking up a place next to the first. This one appeared to be badly injured, however. She had a deep bloodied gash in her torso. It was bleeding so much, it was staining the water.

Mermaids. What are they doing here?

Is there a gate nearby? Somewhere in the water? How else would they have gotten here?

I had left The Shade with a map of gates connecting the human and supernatural realms. Unfortunately, it had later been confiscated by hunters, but I couldn't remember noticing a gate in any seas or oceans. I could only guess that the map was not comprehensive.

The two creatures began punching the glass in unison.

Crap.

In my panic, I performed maneuvers with the submarine that I hadn't thought I was capable of in my continued attempt to throw them off, but it was futile.

"Ben," River gasped. She clutched the arms of her seat with white knuckles. "There's another one."

Sure enough, barely a second later, another slammed against the glass. Now all three pounded away.

I stopped trying to shake them off and this time focused on rising to the surface as fast as I possibly could. As the first crack formed in the glass, we burst up above the waves.

These were fish. I expected them to immediately start gasping and writhing, but they did no such thing. Although their natural habitat was in the water, they could clearly survive for some time above the surface. Encouraged by the crack that had appeared, they beat harder against the glass.

I grabbed River's hand and pulled her out of the

control room, slamming the door behind us.

Gripping her head, I forced her to look me in the eye. "Lock yourself in a cabin. Don't come out until I say. Understand?"

She looked terrified, but nodded and raced away.

A hellish screech assaulted my eardrums as I hurried up the ladder and pushed open the hatch in the roof of the submarine. Hauling myself out into the night, I glared down at the three creatures still clinging to the windscreen. I was furious to see that one of them had managed to punch a fist right through the glass by now. She didn't seem to be at all concerned about the fact that her fist was now a bloody mess. She was still gripping the jagged glass, trying to make the hole bigger.

Extending my claws and baring my fangs, I moved toward them, slashing the nearest one to me across the face. She howled and went tumbling down into the water.

One of the remaining two launched toward me with alarming speed, her hands outstretched and aiming for my foot. I dodged her, and she went rolling off the side of the submarine, back into the sea. The third one—with an injured torso—had now managed to make a hole big enough to slip through. Grabbing hold of a pole so I wouldn't go skidding into the water, I reached for her. She slipped through too quickly, and although I managed to grab the tip of her tail, it was too slippery for me to hold onto.

I was about to slip through after her when a squelching sound came from above me on the roof. Turning to face the open hatch, I was just in time to see a tail disappear through it, and then a loud thud came from inside the submarine.

Damn.

Why the hell do they want to get in our submarine?

Rushing through the open hatch, I laid eyes on another creature squelching away from me across the corridor. But this one looked different than the others. With shorter hair, broad square shoulders, and a thick waist, this was clearly a male.

I caught up with him in a few strides and gripped the back of his neck. He squirmed beneath me and twisted round on his back to look up at me, revealing a face that was no less hideous than the women's. He tried to bite my wrist with his sharp black fangs, but I struck him hard across the face. I was about to slit his throat when I noticed that he was wheezing badly. He looked so ill and pathetic as he lay beneath me, I decided to just leave him there and deal with the other who had made her way toward River's side of the submarine.

Following the trail of dark blood the mermaid had left along the floor, I found her, to my surprise, curled up in a fetal position in a corner of an empty cabin. The fin at the end of her long tail was splayed out to cover her face. Her whole body trembled as she too had begun to make a wheezing sound.

I hurried back along the corridor to fetch the merman and dragged him into the cabin along with the female. I wasn't sure what to do with them. I really didn't want to kill them, but I also didn't see the point in throwing them back in the water when they clearly didn't want to be there. It seemed that they would rather die up here. Locking them both inside, I headed back to the control room to examine the broken screen.

I breathed out in frustration. *Great.* After all the trouble we'd undergone to find a submarine, now we were going to have to spend the rest of the journey above the waves.

I was about to go to River when something outside caught my eye. Bright blue lights. Flashing beneath the surface of the water. Grabbing a pair of goggles from one of the cabinets, I slid out through the hole in the glass and stood at the edge of the submarine. Staring down to the dark waters, I tried to make out what was causing the light. But the moonlight was reflecting too much over the surface.

Lowering myself into the sea, I put on the goggles and dipped down. Beneath the surface I looked toward the direction of where the light seemed to be coming from, and almost swallowed a mouthful of water in shock.

Perhaps a hundred merfolk darted in all directions as blue light shot toward them. Five black submarines were surrounded by dozens of divers in black suits, all armed with some kind of mini torpedo.

River and I needed to get far, far away from here.

I was about to haul myself back onto the submarine when a diver came into view about twenty feet beneath me. He was staring up at me, his head cocked to one side.

Hurrying out of the water and back into the control room, I just prayed that in the few seconds that diver saw me, he had not been able to detect that I was a vampire. I hoped he'd assume I was just a curious onlooker who happened to be passing this way.

I urged the vessel forward as fast as I could in the opposite direction.

"Ben?" River called. "What's going on? Can I come out?"

"Just… stay where you are for now," I replied.

The strong sea wind entered the control room as the sub sped faster and faster. I breathed in a scent that chilled me.

Human blood. Warm human blood. It was close. Too close.

I urged the vessel forward, but it was already going at maximum speed.

I pulled myself through the hole in the screen and

looked round, trying to trace the source of the blood. Then I caught sight of two submarines above the surface, chasing after us.

No.

"Ben? What's going on?" River's voice again.

I didn't answer her.

If those hunters catch up with us, this is the end of our journey. The end of us.

Navigating the submarine, I had been so focused on the two vessels behind me that I only noticed the one in front when its smooth surface emerged from the waves. It was a much larger submarine than ours and was positioned deliberately to block our path. I swerved to the right to avoid it, but the two submarines behind me were fast closing in. As all three worked together to trap us, it became clear to me that it was only a matter of time.

We had two options. Continue to try to skirt away from them in this vessel, the vessel that was much more outdated and slower than their own, or dive into the water.

My guess was that we would survive longer beneath

the water than in such a big, clunky open target. Keeping the submarine speeding on autopilot, I left the control room and raced to River's bedroom. As I opened the door, she looked at me in panic, a line of sweat on her brow.

"What is happening?" she gasped.

I just grabbed her and pulled her toward the ladder. Climbing up, I opened the hatch and raised my head slowly.

A shower of bullets fired at me the second my head came into view. I ducked just in time to avoid being hit by one square in the jaw. *It's too late.* If we were to step out now, we'd be blown to bits within seconds.

I looked down at River. "Hunters. Change of plan," I breathed through gritted teeth, closing the hatch again and pulling her back down the ladder.

As I moved back toward the control room, the sound of the window smashing filled my ears. I didn't need to step inside to realize what must've just happened. The submarine that had been closing in from the front had caught up. As the scent of human blood grew stronger, and footsteps rang on the nose of the submarine, I gripped River's hand and dragged her toward the furthest room away from them. A small bedroom cabin. Locking the door behind me, I looked down at her.

"We're trapped," she whispered.

A beeping had started from the other side of the submarine, and now there were footsteps in the control room. A door swung open.

I focused on River, taking in her face, her eyes, her lips. Bending down, I gripped the sides of her head and kissed her. Hard. She responded, even as her hands trembled as they touched my hair.

"Get underneath the bed," I breathed, as our lips parted.

She lowered to the floor and slid beneath the bed. She was still holding onto my hand, trying to drag me down with her.

"Ben." She looked at me pleadingly.

I shook my head, and detached myself from her.

"They're going to kill you the moment they see you," she whispered.

Maybe. But I was going to try to take a few of them

out before they shut me down. I wanted to make this as difficult for them as possible.

I just looked down at her calmly, taking in her beautiful face for what I was sure would be the last time, and then turned to face the door. The beeping grew closer and closer, as did the footsteps, along the corridor toward us. A few moments later, someone gripped our door handle. It rattled as they began shaking it.

I leapt up to the ceiling, stretching myself out against the walls like a spider, so I would have an advantage over them when they first came in, and more chance of taking a few out before they got to me.

I waited with bated breath as what sounded like several men began to kick the door. Then metal clicked. And a gunshot rang out. A bullet shot right through the door and shattered the mirror at the opposite end of the room. Then came another gunshot, and another, until a circle of holes had been created around the handle. Now all they had to do was kick the door open. Bracing myself in the next few seconds that River and I would have in this cabin alone, I prepared to pounce.

But the door did not budge.

River looked bewildered as she looked from me to the door from the spot she was hiding in beneath the bed.

No hunters stepped through it. Not even after two minutes of waiting.

Is this some kind of a trap?

What in the world are they waiting for?

Even though I had no idea whether it was safe, I slid back down the walls and cautiously peered through one of the holes in the door.

I could hardly believe my eyes.

Strewn about the floor were the still bodies of half a dozen hunters. Each lay in the same position—on their backs, their eyes blank and wide open, gazing up at the ceiling. And their mouths... blood was trickling from them and pooling beneath their heads.

As I pushed the door open, River slid out from beneath the bed and stood next to me.

"What happened?"

"I have no clue," I replied.

"They're dead," she said.

I approached the nearest man to me and felt his pulse, even as his blood called to me.

"Yes. Dead."

I moved along the submarine, checking in other cabins for hunters. Then I climbed up the ladder and poked my head through the hatch. The submarines that had been chasing us had come to a standstill, and as my eyes fell to the water surrounding us, I spotted more bodies floating in the water.

I didn't think that it was possible for me to feel more bewildered, but as I ducked back down into the submarine and entered the control room with River, it was to see that the window was no longer smashed. It was completely repaired, as if it had never been broken to begin with.

CHAPTER 17: Ben

I drained and stored the blood of the dead hunters lying in the corridor, then threw the corpses into the sea. I had been worried about what I was going to do for human blood for the rest of the journey. I didn't need to think about that problem again for a while now.

River and I were still lost for words as we took a seat back in the control room and I started up the submarine again. I stared through the perfectly smooth glass.

I had no idea what had just happened, but when River's and my tattoos started prickling as we dipped beneath the surface of the waves and continued our journey underwater, I couldn't help but link the incident to the last bizarre experience we'd had—blood raining from the sky.

River drew the same conclusion.

"Something is following us," she said, brushing her fingers gingerly over her tattoo.

But what? Neither of us knew how to even begin to speculate. It was all so bizarre. If it were really Jeramiah's witches following us, why would they even bother? If they wanted us to return to The Oasis, they could magic us there by force. Why follow us around and play these mind games with us?

A slapping noise came from the back of the submarine.

I groaned internally.

"We still have those merpeople back there," I muttered.

"What are we going to do with them?" River

asked anxiously.

"Let's go and take a look at them."

Once we had gotten well away from the area where the hunters had been, I put the vessel back on autopilot and the two of us headed to the back of the submarine.

I opened the door of the cabin where we'd left the mermaid and merman. They were curled up together in a corner in the same fetal position.

I walked over to the male and nudged his slimy shoulder. He didn't even look up at me, though he was clearly still alive.

"We can't risk throwing them back in the water again. For some weird reason, they've decided they want to be inside our submarine. If we let them go, they might try to break through the glass again."

"Then what?" River said, frowning. "We just keep them locked in here?"

"Yes. For now," I muttered, leading her back out of the room and closing the door. "It's their stupid fault they climbed in here. I don't have a lot of sympathy for them."

They seemed docile, and they might even die on their own anyway. Those slimy creatures were really the last thing on my mind right now.

We spent some more time in the control cabin while I plotted our course for the rest of the journey, and then we headed to one of the cabins—whose door was broken thanks to the hunters—and sat down on the bed. She leaned back against a pillow, pulling a blanket up around her, while I leaned against the wall.

"Mermaids," she muttered, still looking traumatized. "I feel like I'm ruined."

I shot her a glance. "Ruined?"

"I wanted to be Ariel when I grew up… now that movie will never be the same again."

I smirked. "You still watch that cartoon?"

She poked me in the shoulder. "Don't judge."

She heaved a sigh and we fell into silence. She moved closer to me on the bed. I slid my arms around her as she nestled against my chest.

When she spoke again, it was in a deeper voice. "I honestly thought that we were going to die in this room."

I kissed the top of her head. "So did I."

CHAPTER 18: ROSE

After Caleb agreed to turn me, I promised not to speak of the subject again for the rest of our trip. And I kept my promise.

Our honeymoon turned out to be everything I could have imagined it to be. Having so much uninterrupted time with Caleb was bliss. Just the two of us, adrift in the middle of the ocean. We ended up spending longer at sea than we'd planned before reaching the first island, just because we were so wrapped up in each other's company.

When we finally began stopping at islands, I realized that Caleb hadn't been joking when he'd said that he would take me to remote parts. We hardly spotted a single human. By day, we stayed on the boat, and at night, we roamed the islands. I had also brought a number of small instruments with us from my father's music room. We bathed in hot springs, went on long walks and explored the gorgeous landscapes. Often I would spark up a bonfire and we would sit around it, playing and making up our own melodies. Our nights often ended up with making love on the beach before returning to the boat before the sun rose. Even though Caleb tired me out and we were out all night, I found that I just couldn't sleep much. I just wanted to be with him. And of course, he barely slept anyway.

Once we hit New Zealand, things got more upbeat. Despite agreeing to stay away from humans, we did spend many nights in clubs on the beach, and during the day continued sailing around different parts of the magnificent country.

I took a charmed phone with us, and remembered to call my mother once a week as I had promised to assure her that we were still fine. But time flew by, and before I knew it, we'd been gone several weeks.

Since we had finished touring all the places that Caleb had planned out, he suggested that we start making our way back. We stocked up on food supplies for me with the money we had brought with us, and there was still plenty of blood in the boat's storage room.

And then we took off into open ocean, making our way back toward The Shade.

We traveled slowly. We wanted to make the most of our time away, but I suspected that Caleb was also going slower because he was beginning to feel more and more nervous about the end of the journey, when he'd promised to turn me.

We spent a few more days on the ocean, enjoying the last of our long honeymoon. But finally, we began to near home.

It was close to midnight one night when Caleb felt that we had neared close enough to The Shade. He moored the boat and then looked at me. I couldn't miss the worry in his eyes as I stood with him in the control room.

Taking my hand, he led me out onto the deck. He looked toward the distance, scanning the shoreline. I couldn't see so far into the darkness.

"Do you think those hunter ships are still surrounding The Shade?" I asked.

"We're not close enough to them now to see. But if I had to take a guess, I would say that they are still there."

Gathering me closer to him, he leaned down and closed his mouth around mine, caressing my lips slowly and tenderly. He kissed me as though I was the most precious thing in the world.

Raising his head again, he looked deep into my eyes.

"Are you sure this is what you want?" His voice sounded hoarse.

I swallowed hard. "Yes."

"Because the last thing I want is for you to regret this decision," he said. "You know that it will mean losing your fire powers, right? They will become dormant, like your father's do when he is a vampire."

I raised my hand to his face, my thumbs brushing

either side of his lips as I kissed him harder.

"I want you to turn me, Caleb."

I had grown attached to my fire powers and I was sad at the thought of losing them, but this was what I wanted. Still, the pain and danger of the experience had been built up so much, I couldn't help but feel nervous. But I made sure to not show it in my expression. I didn't want Caleb to see even the slightest bit of hesitation in me, because this was difficult enough for him as it was.

He nodded slowly. "All right."

Taking my hand, he led me down to our bedroom.

"Is this really the best place to turn me?" I asked. "Won't we get the bed all... messy?"

"Yes, it's going to be messy," Caleb said grimly. He had a dark expression as he looked around the room. "But I would rather have you in a contained space than out in the open. I don't know what kind of state you're going to wake up in. The last thing I want is for you to go diving into the ocean."

My spine tingled as he sat me down on the bed.

"Wait here," he said.

I did as he requested. He returned a minute later carrying a large blue tarpaulin. I lifted myself from the bed as he spread it out over the mattress, covering the silk linen.

Then he nodded toward the center of the bed. I positioned myself there and looked up at him, my heart fluttering.

He removed his shirt and dropped it to the floor. Then he climbed onto the bed and crawled toward me. He positioned himself over me until his legs straddled my hips. He unbuttoned my shirt and removed it completely, discarding it on the floor next to his own. Then he removed my jeans. Now I wore only my underwear.

His breath hitched as he positioned himself over me, his eyes falling to my neck.

He placed his hands either side of my head, his fingers tangling in my hair. He lowered his head to mine and caught my lips in his. I could feel how tense he was, and I could feel him trembling slightly. I reached up my hands and cupped his face, hoping to reassure him. When his lips broke away from mine, I whispered:

"I trust you, Caleb."

CHAPTER 19: Caleb

My hands shook slightly as they rested in my wife's hair.

I closed my eyes, relishing the feel of her warm hands against my face. I didn't know when I would feel her heat again.

Rose's sweet scent engulfed me as I dipped down lower. So close to her, normally by now I would be in full-blown battle mode to restrain myself. But this night would be different. For the first time since I had met her, I would taste her blood. I swallowed hard as she stared up at me, her eyes so wide and trusting.

"Just try to keep as still as possible," I said, my mouth dry.

She nodded, and then, after dipping down to taste her lips once more, I moved toward her neck and pressed my mouth against her soft skin. I bared my fangs, feeling her tender flesh beneath them. My mouth salivated. I could practically taste her blood already. I pressed down harder. Rose gasped, her fingers digging into my back as I broke skin.

A hot rush of blood flowed into my mouth, setting my tastebuds alight. Her taste overwhelmed my senses. It was more exquisite than I had imagined. As the blood glided down my throat, my gut clenched. My instinct was to lose myself in her and take draught after draught until I had sucked her dry.

I couldn't stop myself from swallowing three mouthfuls, but after that, I managed to regain control of myself. Forcing myself to focus, I released my venom.

Rose moaned and squirmed.

Lowering a hand to her right thigh, I repositioned

her beneath me as I finished infecting her. And then I withdrew, my mouth dripping with her blood as I raised my head above her. I stared down at my beautiful wife. Her eyes were shut tight, her forehead now covered with a sheen of sweat. Her head rolled from side to side as her convulsions grew stronger and stronger.

And then came the vomiting of blood.

I never would get used to witnessing a turning. The horror of my own was still fresh in my mind, even though it had taken place many decades ago. I would never forget the pain. The fear…

I might not be able to do anything about the pain for Rose, but at least I could help to alleviate her fear.

Moving to the side of the bed, I placed a palm over her forehead and stroked it. I reached for her hand and clasped it tight.

"You're doing fine, Rose," I said calmly. "I'm here with you, and I'm not leaving."

I wasn't sure whether my words registered with her, or whether the pain was all-consuming. But I hoped that the steady sound of my voice would help reassure her.

The waiting that followed was torturous. As promised, I didn't once leave her side. I lost all track of time as I remained in that bedroom with her. My only relief came from seeing that she did not seem to be vomiting more blood than was usual. I had not been there to witness Ben's turning personally, but I had heard from his parents that he had been expelling huge amounts of blood.

When Rose finally began to show signs of consciousness, and she stopped coughing up blood, I wiped her down with a wet towel and placed it over her forehead.

Then she became still.

I removed the pillows from beneath the blood-soaked tarpaulin and piled them up against the headboard. I helped her sit up and leaned her against them.

I kissed her cheek. Her cold, pale cheek.

"Rose," I said gently.

When her eyes flickered open and met mine, I witnessed their vibrancy as a vampire for the first time.

They were a vivid emerald green. Rose's eyes had taken my breath away when she was a human, but now they were all the more stunning. Her dark hair contrasted starkly with her pale skin.

I snapped myself out of admiring her beauty and reminded myself of our next concern.

Had she or had she not woken up like her brother?

I placed my hands on her shoulders. "How are you feeling?" I asked.

She still looked in a daze. Her eyes were slightly unfocused even as they looked up at me. Her lips opened as if she wanted to say something, but then they closed again.

"Rose?" I pressed.

She motioned to sit forward and I let her. Crouching down on all fours on the mattress, she breathed heavily for the next three minutes. Then she looked up and, without warning, leapt off the bed.

Her eyes were wide as she gripped her throat, her expression desperate.

"Caleb," she wheezed. "I need blood."

Grabbing hold of her arm, I pulled her out of the

bedroom and led her into the storage room. There I picked up a large sack of blood and, sitting her down in one corner, opened it and helped her to drink it.

I watched with bated breath as she swallowed mouthful after mouthful in quick succession until she had downed the entire sack of animal blood.

"More," she breathed.

I reached for another sack, and fed that to her too. And then another. And then another. Although she wrinkled her nose in disgust at the taste, she kept drinking more.

I kept expecting her to throw it all up any second now.

But half an hour passed, and nothing happened.

Once she felt that she had consumed enough blood, I took her out of the storage room and led her into the bathroom. Removing her blood-stained underwear, I guided her beneath the shower and soaped her down, removing all traces of blood from her soft, milky skin. She still looked like it hadn't quite sunk in, as though she was in a world of her own. I kept asking her how she was feeling, and whether she was sure that she'd drunk enough blood. She kept replying that she was okay.

After showering her, I dried her and helped her into clean clothes. Then, avoiding the upstairs deck where it was now sunny, I led her into the living area and sat down on the couch with her. I gathered her in my arms and held her close against me.

We passed the next two hours in that way, me talking gently with her and her recovering from the shock and adjusting to her new body.

After five hours had passed and she became thirsty for more animal blood, one truth became apparent to both of us:

There was something seriously wrong with Benjamin.

CHAPTER 20: RIVER

After passing the Philippines and finally entering the Pacific Ocean, I was relieved when Ben said we'd reached the final leg of the journey.

The merfolk remained in the cabin we had allotted for them, and we went to check on them every now and then—more out of curiosity than anything else. They were still alive, though they hardly budged an inch. I wasn't sure what we intended to do with them when we arrived in The Shade, but for now, we didn't have a choice but to keep them with us.

As we entered deeper into the Pacific Ocean, I just prayed that we wouldn't meet with any more obstacles before arriving in The Shade. My prayers weren't entirely answered.

After the fifth day in the ocean, we found ourselves caught up in a hurricane. We'd been forced to surface for fresh air due to a malfunction in the carbon dioxide scrubber, and now Ben struggled to navigate the submarine against the strengthening current. We had to stop for a while and try to weather the storm.

The night when the hurricane was at its strongest, I'd just finished having a shower. The submarine started rocking more than ever. I was terrified that we'd find ourselves stranded in the middle of the ocean.

Ben had already left the control room and by now he had retired to his cabin. Though I was sure that he wasn't sleeping. I didn't know how anyone could sleep through this turbulence.

I turned the corner of his doorless cabin. Sure enough, he was sitting upright in bed with a bunch of maps. He raised his gaze to me as I approached. He gathered up the maps and moved them onto a table, making space for me to sit next to him.

Though I didn't sit. I stretched out my legs and lay on my side, indicating that he do the same.

He looked down at me curiously, then got into the same position. He reached out to touch my face, then ran his hand through my hair.

"You okay?" he asked.

I brushed a thumb over his lips, then moved in to kiss him. It felt like home as his strong body enveloped me and the storm faded into the background.

Despite his coldness, a warmth spread through me as his right hand traveled slowly up and down my back, stroking me, reassuring me.

I shut my eyes tight, listening to the beating of his heart.

Benjamin Novak.

I'd been hoping against hope that we would reach The Shade, but now that we were nearing it, a part of me was dreading it. The Shade marked the end of our journey, possibly the end of us… whatever *us* was. A brief friendship. A sweet romance. Two straws being drawn together in a current and then being pulled apart.

I wasn't sure that I would ever meet another guy like Benjamin Novak. I wasn't sure there *was* another guy like him.

He'd told me that we could still stay in touch, but of course it wouldn't be the same. Being so far apart… we would drift apart eventually. No doubt he would find someone else. Maybe I would too.

I just wished somehow we could stay together, even though I knew that it was impossible if I wanted to see my family again. My family who so desperately needed me.

Still, I found myself voicing my impossible fantasy. "I wish we didn't have to part," I whispered.

He reached for my face and tilted it upward, so that he could look me in the eyes. His green gaze fixed on me. He ran his tongue over his lips, which parted slightly, as if he were about to answer. Then he dipped his head and claimed my lips in a slow, passionate kiss.

"I don't know what the future holds for either of us, River," he said softly. Lifting his face, he looked down on me like I was the most precious thing in the world. "I'm just grateful that, tonight, I have you."

CHAPTER 21: BEN

Thankfully, we got through the hurricane without too much damage to the submarine. After that, the rest of the journey flew by. I kept expecting another obstacle to derail us, but no. We passed the rest of the way smoothly. So smoothly that I was almost suspicious.

I began to feel more and more nervous as we neared the boundary of The Shade. As we reached within several dozen miles, my throat was tight. The night I had murdered Yasmine replayed in my mind, every horrifying detail. I tried to shove the memory out of my mind.

Nothing like that is going to happen this time. I will have River's blood, and I'll stay by the boundary.

As we were closing the distance, I noticed something strange. Five huge gray vessels, evenly spaced around the island.

What are they?

They certainly didn't belong to The Shade. And if they weren't The Shade's ships, whom else could they belong to other than… the hunters?

How would they know The Shade's location?

I sped up the submarine, pushing aside thoughts of the ships as I focused on reaching the boundary.

I raised the top half of the submarine from the water just as we were about to pass through. River stared as what had previously been an expanse of ocean turned into a view of a magnificent dark island as the first half of the submarine entered within the boundary. Part of me was grateful that we had even managed to enter inside. I was worried that something might've caused the spell to wear off and I wouldn't be allowed to enter.

Even the merfolk in the back seemed to sense that

we were entering someplace new, since I felt and heard movement near the back of the submarine as the rest of the vessel passed through the boundary.

Now fully inside, I scanned the length of the shoreline anxiously. Although a part of me was yearning to see my friends and family again, I just was not ready for it yet. I was glad that I couldn't spot anyone on the beach, nor by the Port.

River picked up the container of her blood that she had prepared for me earlier and slipped it into the compartment next to my seat.

"Are you sure that's enough for you?" she asked, eyeing the container nervously.

I looked down at it. "This'll be okay. I won't be hanging around long here anyway."

I was actually surprised by how much blood she'd managed to draw in a short time. Clearly she didn't want a repeat of what had happened in the Egyptian guesthouse.

My heart was pounding by the time we reached the jetty. Taking River's hand, as well as the container of blood, I stopped by the ladder beneath the hatch. I gathered her in my arms and pressed my lips against her neck, drawing in her scent and then kissing her deeply.

Her eyes were glassy as she looked up at me. "I can't believe we're here," she said. "Thank you so much."

She pulled my neck further down and pressed her mouth against mine again.

I held her head in my hands. "I'll see you once more before I leave. Just come to the Port and wave to me—I'll be watching for you. But until then, do you know exactly what to do?" Although we'd already discussed it, I wanted to be sure that she was comfortable.

"Yes," she said. "I need to ask the first person I come across to take me to your parents—Derek and Sofia Novak. I need to say that I'm your friend, and you have sent me here. I need to tell them that you're okay, and ask them to take me to see the witches to help me find a cure."

She looked nervous, even though I had assured her everyone on the island would treat her well. Of course, having told her that this island was packed full of strange supernatural creatures she hadn't come across before—like werewolves and ogres—I couldn't expect her to feel anything but nervous.

She climbed up through the hatch, and closed it behind her. I headed back to the control room and watched as she made her way along the jetty. She entered the clearing, then disappeared into the woods.

I just hoped that, for the sake of her nerves, Brett wouldn't be the first person she came across.

CHAPTER 22: RIVER

I stared around at the dark island in wonder. I could still hardly believe that I was here. The Shade. A mystical island filled with supernaturals, an island I hadn't known even existed until a short while ago.

I walked slowly as I crossed the clearing beyond the Port. All my senses were overwhelmed by the beauty of the place. The fragrance of exotic flowers mixed with the scent of the giant sequoia trees. The ocean breeze against my skin. The whispering of leaves and the chirping of birds. The moon amid a sea of stars, casting down a sheen of pale light.

I'd only set foot on this island for a few minutes, but I already sensed that The Shade was a place of magic. A place of mystery. A place where anything could happen.

Always night. I can't believe it's always night here.

Leaving the clearing and entering the forest, I found myself walking along a path that was clearly well trodden. I looked around wide-eyed, listening for any sounds of someone near me. So far, the noisiest thing was the snapping of twigs beneath my feet.

It felt like I'd been walking for perhaps a mile through the forest when voices drifted toward me from the trees to my right. I squinted, looking toward the source of the noise. Seeing nothing but thick trunks, I left the path and began making my way through the undergrowth.

Peering through the last line of trees, I found myself staring down at a magnificent lake. Standing in an old boathouse were a man and a woman—a pretty woman with long red hair, and a tall dark-haired man wearing glasses.

Going by Ben's description of his mother, I thought for a moment that this might be her, but I soon realized that she wasn't as the man spoke.

"I can't go on like this, Adelle."

Adelle's face was ashen as she looked down at her feet.

"You're bottling something up," the man continued. "I've sensed you have been for the past few months. And I… I can't be with someone who doesn't trust me enough to speak their mind."

The redhead heaved a sigh. "I'm so sorry. I know. It's not fair. I-I've just been so scared to tell you." She reached out and touched his arm. "I don't want to hurt you, Eli. I really don't."

"Just tell me what's on your mind. As long as it's the truth, it doesn't matter if it hurts."

"I… I'm in love with Aiden."

Eli's jaw twitched as he took a step back from her. He swallowed hard, then nodded slightly.

"I guessed as much."

"I thought I could forget about him. I really did. I just… I simply can't."

Eli cleared his throat. "So you've loved him all this time. At least… now we know where we stand. We were living a lie before."

The woman wrapped her arms around Eli and hugged him. "I still care about you so much. I do."

He hugged her back stiffly.

"I hope you won't hold any grudge against Aiden. He's been nothing but honorable. He urged me to come back to you when I left you."

Eli nodded.

Adelle sounded close to tears. "I think I'm going to leave The Shade."

Eli raised a brow. "Leave?"

"Yes. Not forever, but for a while. I need to take some time out… reorient myself."

"Where will you go?"

She bit her lip. "I'm not sure where I'll end up exactly. I'd like to travel a bit."

Eli paused, then said, "I think that's a good idea."

"I'll move my stuff out of your apartment tonight. And I think I'll leave the island tomorrow morning. One of the other witches will have to step in as headmistress while I'm gone."

"Okay… You go ahead and do what you have to do. The front door is open. I need some time alone."

Adelle drew Eli in for another hug, and then—to my shock—she vanished from the spot.

Wow. Could she be… a witch?

Recovering from the surprise, I felt bad for listening in on such a personal conversation, but I needed to speak to someone, and didn't want to interrupt.

Now that this Eli was on his own, I crept out of the trees and approached him.

"Um, excuse me," I said tentatively.

He spun around, and his eyes widened as he looked me over.

He frowned. "Who are you?"

"My name is River. River Giovanni. I'm a friend of Benjamin Novak. He sent me here and I need to speak to his parents, Derek and Sofia. Can you please take me to them?"

His expression turned from surprise to shock. "Y-Yes, of course. But, how on earth did you get here?"

"Ben brought me," I said.

"Ben? He's in The Shade?"

"He's waiting in a submarine just outside the island."

"Follow me," Eli said at once.

Clearly this person was a vampire. He began speeding away too fast for my half-blood legs to keep up.

He stopped when he saw that I was lagging behind, and hung back for me to catch up. "What are you exactly? Your skin is pale like a vampire's, but you're clearly not one."

"I'm a half-blood."

"Half-blood?" he said, peering down at me all the more curiously though his glasses.

"Please, I can explain everything, but I need to speak to Derek and Sofia urgently."—I kept thinking about Ben with my container of blood. I was still having doubts how long that would last him before the human blood of The Shade began calling to him.

"Of course I'll take you there," Eli said. "You might want to climb onto my back though since it will be faster."

I climbed onto the vampire's lean frame and he began racing off into the darkness of the woods. He was so fast it was hard for me to see where we were going, but when he stopped, it was at the foot of a towering redwood tree. But I was confused. This part of the woods seemed just as bereft of vampires as the one that I had left.

"Where—?"

He pointed upward.

I gasped. "Oh, my."

Benjamin had described something of The Shade to me, but he hadn't described these. Stunning penthouses built atop the giant redwood trees.

Wow.

Eli took me to the thick trunk of the tree, and led me toward an elevator shaft that had been hidden round the back. He stepped inside with me, and we ascended the towering tree. It took my breath away to look down and I began to feel dizzy as we arrived at the top. Stepping out of the elevator, we emerged on a gorgeous veranda lined with pretty plant and flower plots. And the view from this height... it was unearthly. A sea of treetops spread out for miles. In the distance was the sparkling ocean and to my right was a sprawling mountain range.

Once I tore my eyes away from the heart-stopping view, we stopped outside a large wooden door.

Eli knocked.

"Sofia! Derek!" he called. "Open up!"

I heard the sound of a door opening inside, and then footsteps. The front door swung open a few seconds later.

Standing before me in the doorway, over six feet tall and wearing blue pajamas, was the spitting image of Benjamin Novak. Except for his eyes, the similarities were stunning.

Although there was something that struck me as odd about this man who could only be King Derek Novak... His skin had a light tan glow to it. He was clearly not the vampire Ben had described him as.

I felt shivers run down my spine as the king's piercing blue gaze settled on me. He looked me over curiously, then back at Eli.

"What is all this? At this time of night?"

Eli looked at me, indicating that I do the talking.

I cleared my throat. "My name is River Giovanni and I'm a friend of your son. I need to speak with you and your wife urgently."

"My son?"

"Yes."

"Where is he?"

"He's, uh, waiting near the island."

Derek spun around, looking over his shoulder and called back into the apartment. "Sofia!"

A pretty redhead in her early to mid-twenties raced to the doorway. This was Ben's mom. She was clearly a vampire.

Her green eyes—so similar to Ben's—widened as she stared at me.

"This is River, a friend of Ben," Derek said. "He's near The Shade."

"Where?" she gasped.

"By the boundary near the Port," I said. "I can—"

Before I could finish my sentence, Sofia reached for my hand and pulled me toward the elevator. Derek followed a few feet after, and so did Eli. We all descended in the elevator, and as we reached the bottom, we began running forward, Sofia still holding my hand. I slowed her down considerably compared to the two men who were speeding ahead, but finally we all arrived at the Port.

They stared out over the waves toward the boundary, squinting. I stood at the end of the jetty, looking in the direction I had last seen Ben. At first I thought that he might have left already, and my heart sank, but then I noticed the submarine's shiny roof above the water and the small bump of the hatch.

"Over there." I pointed.

"Ben!" Sofia began to shout.

Derek was already in one of the boats that surrounded the jetty, and we all bundled in after him. We began speeding toward Ben's submarine, which was rising higher above the water.

I knew that Ben would've preferred to leave quietly, but there really wasn't a way around it. Of course they would want to see him. From what Ben was telling me, it had been a long time since they had last seen each other.

I looked nervously at Derek as we neared Ben's submarine.

"Um, I'm not sure that it will be safe for you to go near him," I said. "He still has a problem controlling himself around human blood."

Derek didn't slow down in the slightest, but he looked at me and nodded.

As we reached the submarine, the four of us climbed onto the roof. The hatch lifted and Ben climbed out of it.

"Ben!" his parents called.

The expression on Ben's face was a mixture of tension and confusion. As Derek and Sofia moved toward him, he said, "Dad? You're a… a human? Don't come near me!"

Sofia had already reached him by now, and she embraced him.

I hurried up to Ben and stood right by him, hoping that my blood would help to diffuse the scent of his father.

Derek looked pained as he stared at his son, as though there was nothing more that he wanted to do than pull him in for a hug, but he seemed to know better than to draw too close.

He remained standing at a distance, watching his son.

Sofia had tears dripping down her cheeks as she finally stepped back from Ben. Tears of happiness. Tears of relief.

Ben reached for me, and pulled me closer. His body felt so tense—the effect that his father's blood was having on him. Ben lowered his face to my neck, and breathed me in.

I had a suspicion that he might have already finished the container of my blood while he'd been waiting, perhaps more out of nerves than necessity.

Derek and Sofia looked from Ben to me, then back to Ben.

Then they both asked:

"What happened to you?"

CHAPTER 23: BEN

It would have been less painful not to see my parents, but I could hardly expect them to not come running when River told them how she got here. My gut clenched as soon as my father came within proximity. It was a harrowing feeling. Had River not been here with me, there would have been nothing stopping me from launching at him and trying to sink my fangs into his throat. It was a chilling reminder of the monster I'd become, and why I so desperately needed to find a solution.

Why is my father a human? The question kept running through my mind, more out of fear than curiosity.

When my parents asked what had happened to me all this time, I was not sure how to answer. I felt extremely uncomfortable standing so close to my father, even with River by my side.

"I've been... all over."

"Start from the beginning," my father said.

The beginning. It seemed like an age had passed since I'd first left The Shade on the submarine, hoping against hope that my lust for human blood would subside and I would able to stomach animal blood. Those days of optimism, when I'd thought that I might still learn to control myself around humans, had long passed.

"I understand why you choose not to set foot on the island," my mother said, "but why don't you come and sit in our boat? It'll be more comfortable than standing on this roof."

I was still nervous about getting any closer to my father. But I figured that if River sat on my lap, I would be okay. Besides, Eli and my mother were here to help restrain me if something did go horribly wrong.

My father, mother and Eli stepped onto the boat before me, and then I followed with River, both of us keeping to the far end of the vessel. I pulled River onto my lap, practically smothering her again. I realized how odd this must have looked to my parents.

"River is a half-blood," I said, clenching my jaw and trying to steady my breathing. "That means that she is half human, half vampire. Mom and Eli, I'm sure you can smell that her blood is not at all appealing. Because it's spiked with vampire venom. River is the reason I'm not launching at you now, Dad." I cast my father a glance.

"How did River become a half-blood?" he asked, frowning in confusion. "And how did you two meet?"

I started from the beginning. They all remained quiet as I told them my story, from the night I'd left The Shade, to floating in the ocean in the submarine, to the murders that I'd committed on land, to meeting Jeramiah and my time spent in The Oasis, and finally our bizarre journey back to the island.

They all looked dumbstruck by the time I was finished.

"Lucas had a son," my father said, his jaw hanging open. I wasn't sure how much he had absorbed of my story after I'd revealed Jeramiah's identity. He seemed stunned by this news—just as I had been when I had first found out. "I mean," he continued, "I guess I shouldn't be surprised. Lucas was incorrigible when it came to young women even before he became a bloodsucker. But for him to have a son who is still alive today as a vampire… I never would have dreamt it."

My mother seemed more concerned by the tattoos etched into my and River's arms. She eyed us worriedly.

"Are the tattoos hurting you right now?" she asked.

"Mine isn't hurting… It's giving off a mild prickling sensation. What about you, River?" I asked.

"Mine isn't hurting either," River replied. "Just a prickling."

"And the voices in your head, Ben?" my mother said. "Do you hear them now?"

I shook my head. "Not at the moment."

"Half-bloods…" Eli muttered, his eyes fixed on River. "I have never heard of such a concept."

"Somehow, Jeramiah and his coven discovered that it was possible," I said. "They keep many half-bloods as slaves, though they make lovers out of them too. They are not as strong as vampires, but they are longer-lasting companions than humans—immortal, apparently."

They continued asking me questions to clarify various parts of my story, and finally I found the opportunity to state the actual reason for my return.

"I came back only because of River. I need you to take her to the witches and try to find a cure for her. Her home is in New York and she wants to return to her family there. Assuming the witches find a cure, one of them needs to transport her back home. And if they can't… Then I guess she's going to have to stay here with you in The Shade. It's the only safe place for her."

"But where would you go from here, Ben?" my mother asked. "It's such a different world out there now. Did you see those ships?"

"Yes."

"They're hunter ships, in case you didn't guess," my father said, grimacing toward the vessels beyond the boundary. "Also, I'm not sure if you're aware that your killing in Chile was caught on camera. It was broadcast all over mainstream television."

My jaw dropped. I had been trapped in The Oasis for so long, I hadn't exactly had a chance to follow the news. "It was broadcast on television?"

"Oh, my, I saw that on the news, Ben!" River said. "It didn't click that it was you... the footage was blurry."

"Yes. Quite a bit of footage has been broadcast recently," my father said. "Supernaturals are now entering the consciousness of mainstream human society."

"You were the trigger for all this," Eli said to me. "You broke the code of secrecy."

A feeling of guilt swelled in my stomach. All this time, I'd been totally oblivious to it.

My mother reached for my hand. "What's done is done. There is no point lamenting the past. But now... Benjamin, you need to think carefully about what you're going to do. Neither your father or I are going to stop you if you choose to leave, but I urge you to consider if that is really necessary. If you don't feel confident enough to stay on the island, remember that we could always fix you up a residence on the water here, near the outskirts of the boundary."

"Even that wouldn't be safe," I said. "It's only because of River's blood..." I stopped short, the obvious whacking me over the head like a sledgehammer. "I... I should try to turn into a half-blood."

All four of them stared at me. I could see the penny dropping. I'd already explained to my parents and Eli that half-bloods were immortal, they were harmless without claws and fangs... and they didn't crave blood like vampires did.

"Maybe I just need to forget about the reason I'm like this, and just solve the damn problem at the root."

My mother's face lit up. "Yes. Yes," she said breathlessly. It was clear that she would agree to anything at all if it meant keeping me in The Shade.

My father stood up, looking down at me

thoughtfully. "You would take the cure, and turn back into a human," he said, thinking through my plan out loud. "Then we would need a newly-turned vampire to half-turn you, correct? We don't have any newly-turned vampires on the island right now, at least not to my knowledge." He looked at my mother and Eli. "Do you know of any?"

They both shook their heads.

"So we would have to think about how to handle that," my father continued. "Whether anyone who is already planning to turn would mind doing it a bit sooner than intended…"

"Dad, why are you human?" I finally asked the question that had been bugging me from the moment I laid eyes on him.

He exchanged glances with my mother. "We'll need to explain the whole story for you to understand, and that's going to take hours. But basically, I needed my fire powers back."

"Well, don't you plan to turn back into a vampire?" I asked.

"Yes, at some point… But not yet. I want to hold off

a little longer because, as I discovered the last time I took the cure, you can only take it so many times before you start building up an immunity to it. Things almost went… wrong. So this time when I turn back into a vampire, I want to be sure that I will not need to become a human again."

"We will just have to try to find someone else on the island who wants to turn into a vampire," my mother said.

"What if you still craved human blood even as a half-blood?" River asked me, raising a brow.

"I wouldn't be equipped with a body designed to kill," I said. "I'd be easier to control. And hopefully, the craving would be far less strong and I'd be able to eat normal food, like you can."

"How do you half-turn a person exactly?" Eli asked, still looking fascinated by the concept.

"I've done it twice so far, but I'm hardly an expert. Basically the advice Jeramiah gave me was to dig in your fangs, focus on releasing venom, but then pull back before you feel like you've really started… Yes, I know it sounds vague."

"Okay," my mother said slowly, looking relieved. "So we have a plan. I'll speak to some people tomorrow morning and try to find someone who would be willing to turn soon and then half-turn you. First, of course, you're going to need to take the cure. I think you'll want to rest a bit before that though… you've heard all about how painful it is." She shuddered just at the thought.

Yes, I'd been told how painful it was supposed to be. But I was willing to undergo any kind of pain if it meant solving my problem once and for all.

At least I had some peace of mind now that we had a plan, which was more than I'd had just an hour ago. Heck, more than I'd had since I left The Shade.

Now that I was able to relax a little more, I leaned back in my seat, my hands resting on River's lap rather than gripping her waist as I had been doing.

"Where's Rose?" I asked. "And what's been happening here in The Shade since I've been gone? The black witches? Are they still a threat?"

My mother smiled broadly at me. "Rose is on her honeymoon."

I almost jolted River from my lap. "Honeymoon? What! With whom?"

"With Caleb," my mother said.

"Jesus. They hit it off fast," I said.

"Well, it had been a year… A very intense year."

Once the shock started to wear off, I was filled with a feeling of melancholy.

I missed my sister's wedding.

I wondered what else I had missed.

"When will Rose and Caleb return?" I asked.

"They're due back any day now. They're actually a little late… You have no idea how much Rose has missed you."

"I've missed her too," I said.

"You're also going to have a cousin soon," my father said. "Or should I say, *another* cousin. Vivienne's pregnant. It won't be much longer before she's due. Claudia and Yuri are due for a baby too. Liana and Cameron returned—only recently, actually. Oh, and your grandfather hooked up with a werewolf."

My head reeled. "My God. I really have missed a lot."

"As for the witches," my father continued, "they are no longer a threat. We managed to finish them off."

"How on earth did you do that?"

I insisted that my parents do the same thing that I had done—start from the very beginning, tell me everything that had happened since I had left the island.

When they had finally finished, I felt overwhelmed. I was amazed at how much everyone in The Shade had grown during recent events, especially my sister. *Dragon-pacifier? Fire-wielder? Who would've thought?*

"I wonder whether I possess hidden fire powers as a human," I said.

"It's possible. You can try to summon them after you take the cure," my father said.

"And what about these tattoos?" River asked, rolling up the sleeve of her robe. "And this weird echoing in our ears? Will we just have to learn to live with it, or could your witches do something about it?"

"I suggest we get Corrine and Ibrahim to see the two of you first thing in the morning," my father said. "We can talk to them about finding a cure for you, and also see if they have any ideas on what could have happened to you and Ben in The Oasis—"

"What the—" Eli exclaimed as his eyes fixed on the submarine behind us.

I turned around to see two heads poking out of the hatch. The mermaid and merman. Their scaly faces looked dry and shriveled as they placed one hand after another on the slippery roof of the sub and squelched out.

"Merfolk!" my parents gasped at once.

Before any of us could stop them, they'd slid off the side of the submarine and plopped into the ocean.

"Damn it!" My father looked furious as he stared down into the water. "What were you doing with those in your sub?"

I realized I'd forgotten to tell him that we still had them in the vessel.

"I didn't know what else to do with them. If I let them back into the water while we were still outside The Shade, I was worried they were going to try to smash up the submarine again."

"They had better not try to harm our humans," my

mother said, looking anxiously down at the waves. After their adventures in The Cove, she had experienced firsthand that merfolk were not the cuddliest of creatures.

As we stood watching the two green shadows swim further up the shore and fade beneath the water, Eli muttered what I guessed all of us were thinking:

"This place is turning into a zoo."

CHAPTER 24: BEN

My father said that he would ask one of our witches—or perhaps even Micah—to track down the merfolk tomorrow and expel them outside of the boundary. We had absolutely no reason to show mercy to them, certainly not when it came with a risk to our humans. We already had the occasional shark problem on Sun Beach, and the last thing we needed was a couple of nasty merfolk.

We continued talking some more as each of us remembered details we had missed out in the initial recounting of our stories, and then my parents left for all of us to get some rest. They said that they would come to meet us at the submarine in the morning around 9am.

That left River and me with some time to ourselves. Inside the submarine wasn't an appealing place to sleep that night, to say the least, thanks to the fishy smell the merfolk had released after breaking free from their cabin. Although it wouldn't be as safe as being inside the submarine where the smell of human blood would be less, we decided to lie on the roof of the submarine. As long as I kept River close to me, I was confident I'd be all right. We dried the flattest part of the submarine's roof with towels, then spread out spare blankets to make it comfortable and lay down beneath the stars.

We lay on our sides facing each other. My arm was wrapped around her, keeping her close to me to ensure she didn't roll off into the water during her sleep.

As I took in her beautiful face, something had caught my attention before arriving in The Shade, but now that we were alone again, I noticed it even more.

She appeared… luminous. Her eyes sparkled. Even her skin seemed to have a dewy glow, despite its paleness.

"You're glowing," I whispered, brushing my fingers against her cheek.

"I feel like I'm glowing," she whispered back, her hands resting against my chest. "I've still hardly seen any of this island so far, but something about this place… It lights me up."

"I'm glad you like it here."

She twisted onto her back, my arms still around her, and looked up at the sky. Something seemed to be bothering her as she bit her lip.

"What?" I asked.

"You say you have a lot of humans here," she said. "You even have a school?"

"Yes."

"I just… I just wonder, what if my family moved here?" Her words hung in the air before she added quickly, "I mean, I have no idea if my mother would agree, but this place is paradise. Especially compared to where we live. I know that my sisters would love it here, and my brother… I'm sure all this fresh air would do him good… Of course I don't know whether you just allow anyone to come and stay here."

I smiled. "You're not just anyone, River. Of course your family would be welcome… But would you want to stay here as a human, or as a half-blood?"

"I-I don't know. I mean, it's just too early to say. I'd first need to go to my family and tell them about this place, bring them to visit so they can see for themselves how gorgeous it is, and then think about exactly what I'm gonna do after that…" She paused, grinning. "Who knows, maybe my family would end up wanting to become vampires, or werewolves…"

I chuckled. "It's not possible to become a werewolf. They could become vampires, or even half-bloods, like yourself."

She breathed out, and let out a nervous laugh. "I can't believe we're even having this conversation. My mom, she's like the most skeptical person there is. She might have a heart attack if I brought her here… But I'm also sure, if she opened her mind and saw how beautiful the place was, she'd fall in love with it just as I have."

I reached for the side of her face and pulled her back toward me, planting a gentle kiss on her lips.

"Then stay," I whispered.

"I've never been so excited about an idea in my life," she breathed. "But… If I decide to remain a half-blood, just for now, how will I even return to my apartment to meet my family? Will it be safe?"

"You would return to your apartment with one of our witches, and you'd first scope out the place to check if there were any hunters around. It's quite possible there are hunters keeping tabs on the place in case you return… But if there aren't, you'll be safe spending an hour or two there to convince your mother."

She paused. "Would you come with me on that short visit? After you've turned back into a human, of course. I just think that meeting you—none other than the prince of The Shade—might help me to convince her."

I gave her a funny look. "Why's that?"

"Because you're… awesome?"

"Okay…" I said. "I'm not going to question that."

She giggled. Then we both fell quiet for a while, absorbed in our own thoughts.

"So if I've decided to hold off turning back into a human for now," she said, "that means we can leave aside finding me a cure for the time being, and tomorrow all our focus can be on fixing you."

A wave of relief flowed through me at the thought of finally escaping this hell. I caught River's eye. "You do realize tonight is the last night you'll spend with me as a vampire? I'll soon be a human, and then a mere half-blood... will I still be sexy to you?"

She laughed. Moving her mouth close to my ear, she whispered, "You'll always be sexy to me, Prince... But for now, I'm going to enjoy you as a hunky vampire while I can." And then she closed her lips around mine once again.

CHAPTER 25: ROSE

Staring at myself in the bathroom mirror, I still couldn't believe that I was finally a vampire. I examined my pale skin beneath the warm lighting. I tilted my head back and bared my fangs, watching as they extended as far as they could. And then I looked down at my fingers as I flexed my claws.

It felt like being… some kind of wild animal. I guessed that was what vampires were—animals of sorts. I'd never thought of them that way until now. I could see why vampires became brooding and moody. To suddenly be a beast with a human's brain... It was enough to mess with anyone's head.

Nothing could describe the pain of the turning. At one point, I'd found myself begging to die. I was just grateful that my beloved Caleb had stayed by my side the whole time. I could see from his face how traumatic watching me turn had been for him.

And after the turning had come the hunger, the burning in my stomach—I'd thought my appetite might never be satisfied. I was certain as soon as I felt it that I must have the same problem as my brother. But when I found myself able to consume animal blood, I soon realized that, no—that symptom was normal.

Which meant something about Ben made him totally abnormal. At least now we knew. However small, it was a step in the right direction.

I was thirsty a lot after that first day. It took a lot of getting used to the idea of never chewing and swallowing, but only drinking. It was so boring to only crave the same thing every single day—a gooey red liquid that I previously would have felt ill from putting in my mouth. Now, it was all I wanted.

Caleb insisted that we stay on the water for several days after my turning. He said that I would be a danger to humans around the island if we returned too soon, and it was better to wait this out while we were still in the ocean.

Standing in the bathroom that morning, on the sixth day after my turning, I was horrified to catch myself having a graphic daydream involving a soft human neck and lots of warm blood.

I've turned into a psycho.

This was a recurring fantasy I had during the day. It popped into my head completely uninvited and uncalled for. Caleb told me that it was absolutely normal, and he'd had such thoughts on a regular basis every day while I was still a human. *God, no wonder he was so tense around me.*

Caleb stepped inside the bathroom. He wore a loose shirt with the sleeves rolled up to his elbows and the buttons undone over his chest—his usual attire when we were lounging around on the boat, when he wasn't shirtless, of course.

"I just had another fantasy," I said, eyeing him in

the mirror.

A smile curved his lips. He approached behind me, my back against his chest, and placed a hand either side of me on the counter, pressing me up against it.

His mouth hovered next to my ear.

"So did I," he whispered, his lips grazing my earlobe. "But I suspect that it was quite different from yours…"

I giggled. I could tell that there was a part of Caleb that definitely preferred me as a vampire. Despite his love of my warmth, he could finally relax around me for the first time. I could appreciate only now that I was a bloodsucker myself how much effort he had put into controlling himself around me all the time. I doubted I would've had as much self-control if he were a human.

He caught my hand, and the two of us left the bathroom and went up onto the deck. It was early morning, and the sun was just about to peek out above the horizon.

"I think we can return today," he said.

I shot him a look. "Are you serious? I'm still daydreaming about ripping through jugulars."

"As a vampire, those thoughts never go away," he replied. "They will always be there, especially around humans. I suspect even your mother has thoughts like that from time to time. The only thing you can do is learn to control the urge. Your most dangerous stage has passed. Now's the time to start practicing. Staying on this boat any longer won't make a difference."

I took in a deep breath. "Okay… If you say so. But I'm counting on you to snap my neck if it looks like I'm going to pounce on someone."

He rolled his eyes. "I don't need to snap your neck to get you under control."

I cocked my head to one side. "Oh, really?"

He raised a brow. "Yes. Really."

"Why don't you try me?"

He chuckled, then cast his eyes around the deck. "Okay, vampire," he said, setting his eyes on a mast near the bow of the boat. "Pretend that mast is a human. Rush to attack it. I'll give you a head start."

"I don't need a head start."

"Okay…"

I narrowed my eyes on Caleb, then fixed my gaze on

the mast and lurched forward. I had come within two feet of it when Caleb wrapped his arms around my waist, dragging me backward. I tried to tear myself away from his grasp, but no matter how much I struggled, I couldn't. He twisted me to face him, a hint of amusement in his eyes as he wrestled me to the ground. Pinning me against the deck with my arms above my head, he dipped his head down to kiss my lips.

"Do you surrender?" he whispered.

"Never!" I breathed, still struggling even as I returned his kiss.

Before I realized what he was doing, his right hand had crept beneath my arm and he began to tickle me mercilessly, his other hand still holding my wrists over my head.

"No!" I gasped, laughing hysterically. "Cheater!"

He stopped tickling beneath my arms, and instead moved down to my next most ticklish spot, my inner thighs.

After five more minutes of torture, I gave in. He released me, and I stood, my knees feeling wobbly from the trauma he'd just put me through.

"You played dirty," I said, glaring at Caleb as I backed toward the edge of the boat.

"Nobody likes a sore loser, Rose," he said, following me.

As I reached the edge of the ship, I grabbed his hands and pulled him flush against me. I claimed his lips and kissed him passionately, letting my fangs graze gently against his lower lip. He groaned softly. He always seemed to like it when I did that.

I had him too wrapped up in me for him to notice what I was preparing to do. Kissing him harder, I switched position so that he was the one with his back against the edge of the boat. With one swift motion, I pushed him backward into the ocean.

There was a splash. I looked over the edge to see him surfacing a few moments later, his dark hair sopping wet and slicked back away from his face.

He didn't know how sexy he looked when he was wet.

His eyes glinted dangerously.

"Oh, baby. You have no idea what trouble you've

just gotten yourself into."

Leaping from the water, he grabbed me and pulled me back down into the ocean with him. The cool waves engulfed me as Caleb pulled me down deeper and then emerged with me above the surface.

His arms enveloped me as I ran my hands through his hair. His mouth pressed against mine, his tongue pushing between my lips.

I began unbuttoning his shirt. "I'm ready for your trouble, Achilles."

* * *

As the first rays of the sun hit the ocean, Caleb and I climbed back aboard the boat, our clothes flung over our shoulders. We hurried inside before the sun could reach us. I had not yet experienced the pain that the sun caused vampires, and I was in no hurry to.

We took a long shower together and enjoyed washing each other's hair before getting dressed. I looked at him across the bathroom floor as I combed my hair.

"Well. I guess our honeymoon is over now."

I expected him to say something cheesy to make me giggle, like every day was a honeymoon when he was with me. Instead he just smiled, confident in the fact that I knew that he was thinking something along those lines.

We headed up to the control room, where Caleb needed to concentrate. When we got closer to The Shade, we spied five gray hunter ships. They seemed to be at the same distance as before, no closer, no further.

What do they want?

Caleb sped up the boat, not paying too much attention to the ships, except the odd glance to check they had not started moving. And then we passed through the boundary. We were back in The Shade. Back home.

I looked toward the Port, a warm feeling rushing through me, as it did whenever I returned to this island. Although I couldn't have enjoyed our honeymoon more, I loved our island more than anywhere else in the world.

A strong gust of wind blew against me, bringing with it a scent that made my stomach clench. Human blood. *Ugh. What I wouldn't give to take a gulp out of Becky…*

Caleb eyed me, already knowing what I was going through. He squeezed my knee. "You'll be fine. I promise." Then, clearing his throat, he changed the subject. "So when do you want to go see your parents and show them what I've done to you?"

"Oh, yeah…" I'd forgotten about that. I was not entirely sure how my parents might react. Of course, they would be shocked at first, but I wasn't sure if they would be angry, or perhaps understanding of why I had made this choice. I hoped that it would be the latter.

"We might as well go see them first thing. I don't see the point in delaying it."

"Wait a minute," Caleb said, his head craning to our right.

He pointed to what looked like the roof of a submarine poking above the waves. It was floating in the distance within the boundary, and resting on top were two figures. I moved out onto the deck, my vampire vision coming in handy.

Yes. It was a man and a woman, lying together on

the roof of the submarine. Though I couldn't see their faces, because their heads weren't turned in my direction.

"Let's go see who they are," I said, suddenly anxious.

I wondered if perhaps they were injured. Why would they just be lying out on a submarine like that?

We moved closer, until finally, I was at the right angle to see their faces.

I had no idea who the girl was—I didn't recognize her as a resident of The Shade, though she looked pale enough to be a vampire—but when my eyes settled on the young man, I was so shocked that I screamed.

"Ben!"

CHAPTER 26: BEN

I was woken by someone screaming my name. I sat bolt upright, my eyes fixed on my sister, standing in a boat and staring at me.

I shot to my feet, gaping at her. I wondered for a moment whether I was dreaming.

"Rose," I choked. "You're… a vampire?"

Leaping from her boat, she landed on the submarine's roof. She launched into my arms, the force of her jump almost sending me staggering back into the water.

I hugged her tight as she squeezed me back even tighter. She kissed my cheek furiously, practically shaking against me.

"Ben! Where have you been? What happened to you? How come you're back?" Question after question flowed from her mouth before I could come up with a single answer.

I was still in too much shock to see her as a vampire. My brain was too flooded with my own questions and doubts, I was struggling to make room for hers.

"You're a vampire," I repeated, staring at her, dumbstruck. "Mom or Dad turned you?"

She shook her head. "Caleb did. But what—?"

"Are you able to drink animal blood?" I asked, gripping her shoulders.

"Yes," she said impatiently. "The reason I turned was because I wanted to find out if I would have the same problem as you. And I don't, Ben. I can stomach nonhuman blood."

My lips parted, her words sinking in.

Then what is wrong with me?

Caleb stepped out onto the deck of the boat Rose

had just leapt from.

He smiled at me. "Hello, Benjamin."

"Hello, brother-in-law," I said.

Rose's eyes sparkled. "How come you know?"

"I've already spoken to Mom and Dad. They filled me in on everything that's happened since I left. Congratulations." I pulled my sister in for another hug and kissed her cool forehead. "I hate that I missed your wedding."

"I hate it too," Rose said, looking hurt. "You've no idea how much I've missed you."

Rose's gaze traveled to River, who was sitting up on the blankets and watching us.

"Who are you?" Rose asked.

"This is River," I said, reaching a hand down to River and pulling her up to stand next to me. "She's my friend." I was about to add that she was also a half-blood, but that would just invite another onslaught of questions, and I still had a huge backlog to start answering.

And so the four of us gathered on Rose and Caleb's boat and sat around on the deck. I started my story from the very beginning and told it through to the end for my sister and Caleb. They displayed similar reactions to my parents, asking the same questions and looking concerned when River and I showed them our tattoos.

It was strange to have been away from my sister for so long. It had been the longest separation in our life. We'd both had such different experiences, and grown in different ways apart from each other.

I understood why she had wanted to turn into a vampire. And I also understood why my parents hadn't wanted to turn her. After what had happened to me, I wouldn't have wanted her undergoing the risk either. But my sister wasn't one to shy away from danger or risk. Although it unnerved me that something was so different about me, it didn't bother me as much as it should have, because we had a plan now. I was going to become a half-blood.

A part of me was actually grateful that Rose had turned. I'd been dreading our meeting because I'd feared how much her blood would call to me. Now that she was a vampire, I could relax around her.

Once I'd come to the end, Rose walked over to River and kissed her cheek. "Welcome to The Shade," she said, squeezing her hand.

"Thank you." River beamed. I could see that my sister's gesture meant a lot to her.

"No, thank *you* for helping my brother."

From the glance Rose gave me as she sat back down in her seat, I could tell that she'd already figured out that I felt more for River than just friendship.

"So," Caleb said, looking at me, "the plan is for you to turn back into a human today?"

"Yes," I replied.

"And then turn into a half-blood."

"How soon that happens will depend on how soon we're able to get a…" My voice trailed off. My eyes shot toward my sister. "Rose, you could half-turn me."

CHAPTER 27: ROSE

My eyes widened as I stared at my brother. "Are you serious? I—I only just turned. I don't feel confident that I wouldn't just rip out your throat."

"The only vampire who can turn me is one who was just newly turned," Ben replied. "You need to try for me, Rose. You don't have the problem around humans that I do, you'll be as good as anyone."

I looked at Caleb nervously then back to my brother. "Once you're a human, I… I'll think about it," I said.

"Your parents are here," River said, looking toward the Port.

I spun around to see that she was right. My mother and father were sailing toward us on a boat.

"Oh, no," I murmured, "Dad's a human." The first human I encountered in The Shade and wanted to suck dry was my own father. I clutched Caleb's knee, then looked toward my brother and River. He had reached for her and sat her on his knee as he looked out toward our parents approaching in the boat.

"You're going to be okay," Caleb said to me. "You are strong enough to control yourself now."

And yet as my father drew closer and closer, I did not feel strong at all. I sat next to my brother and River in the far corner of the boat, trying to breathe in River's scent so that my father's blood would not be so alluring to me.

"Stop hogging River all to yourself," I said to my brother, managing a grin even as my stomach tensed up in knots.

River chuckled, then lowered her arm to me and allowed me to hold it. I leaned closer to her and took a deep breath.

The fact that my brother had called her just a "friend" was amusing to me. I knew him too well to not notice the way he looked at her, how much he seemed to adore her.

As my parents reached the boat, I braced myself for the explosion.

My mother was the first to lay eyes on me. Her expression of joy at seeing me again soon turned to shock, then horror, as she realized what I had become.

"Rose! You… turned?" She clasped a hand over her mouth, then leapt onto our boat and rushed up to me. Holding my head in her hands, she examined me closely as if wanting to believe that her eyes were deceiving her.

My father's jaw dropped as he saw me. He took a step closer and my whole body tensed up. The demon inside of me clawed for release. I could practically feel the hot blood pumping through his veins.

I imagined how bizarre this experience must have been for my father. His own son and daughter were doing everything they could to not launch at him and drain him dry.

I was used to the abnormal, having grown up on an island of supernaturals, and after everything we had recently been through there wasn't a lot that could faze me these days. But this... This was weird.

Exhaling slowly, I remembered what Caleb had told me.

I can do this. I'm strong enough.

Thankfully, my father didn't step forward as close as my mother did, wisely realizing what I was going through. He looked from me to Caleb, then back to me.

"This was my idea," I said quickly, not wanting them to think that Caleb might have influenced my decision. "Caleb was completely against it."

"Why?" was the one word that spilled from my parents' gaping mouths.

I explained my reasoning. How I had wanted to know if I would have the same problem as Ben, so I could know how this would affect my and Caleb's future, and also to bring us one small step closer to understanding what might be wrong with Ben.

"So you're certain that you don't have the same problem?" my mother asked.

"Yes, positive. I'm not showing any of the signs that Ben showed."

"Why didn't you discuss it with us before you left?" my father asked. "Why do it so suddenly?"

"I just… I thought it best that I just do it. And the most logical time for me to turn was while we were away. We enjoyed our honeymoon, and then we hung around near the outskirts of The Shade while I recovered for the last few days."

"She's all right, Derek," Caleb said. "Give her a few weeks, and she'll live among humans just as well as the rest of the vampires on this island."

Caleb's words seemed to pacify my parents.

My mother held my hands. "Well, as long as you're happy with your decision. It will mean you and Caleb taking the cure and turning back into humans if and when you decide you want children…"

"I know," I said. "I've already thought about it."

"I just wonder why Ben has a problem and you don't," my father said, voicing the question that had been at the back of my mind ever since I turned into a vampire.

"I wonder if something could have happened in Aviary," my mother said, her face tense.

I looked at Ben, who appeared just as clueless as the rest of us.

"I just don't know…"

CHAPTER 28: RIVER

After Benjamin's parents had recovered from the shock of seeing their newly married daughter as a vampire, all of us traveled to the shore. Rose and Ben sat close to me, as far away from Derek as possible. As we reached the Port, Derek stepped off first and distanced himself from the twins, and then I stepped out with them. Ben had an arm around my waist, while Rose had linked her arm with mine. I couldn't help but chuckle at the way both were clinging to me.

Sofia looked at Benjamin. "Are you sure you're

ready for the cure?" she asked.

"As ready as I'll ever be," Ben replied grimly.

"Then I suggest we go straight to the Pit and get this over with," Sofia said. She looked up ahead toward her husband. "Derek, why don't you go and fetch some witches… Ibrahim and Corrine?"

Derek nodded, and then headed off into the woods.

"What's the Pit?" I asked, part intrigued, part chilled by the name.

"You'll see," was all Ben replied.

"We should travel around the outskirts of the island rather than going through the woods," Sofia said. "That way we'll stay further away from the humans… Will you come with us, Rose and Caleb?"

"Of course I'm coming," Rose said, as though it was a stupid question. She glanced at Caleb. "You coming too?"

"Yes, I'll come."

And so we began to run along the borders of the island. Truth be told, I enjoyed every moment of it, admiring the scenery we passed by, until we reached the borders of a mountain range. We climbed over rocks, winding in and out of boulders.

"This area used to be called the Catacombs," Ben said to me. "It's where The Shade used to house its humans, or should I say imprison... Things have changed a lot since then."

Arriving in an area sheltered by rocks, we stopped outside a gated entrance.

"Through there," Ben said, still addressing me as he nodded toward it, "is the only place on the island other than Sun Beach where the sun shines through. It was once used as a torture chamber, to punish vampires who didn't abide by The Shade's law. Now, it's where all vampires who wish to turn back into humans come and lock themselves... It's where you will come if you ever decide you want to turn back into a human and we manage to figure out a cure for half-bloods."

"How long does it take vampires to turn back?" I asked.

"It varies from vampire to vampire... But it's in the hours, not minutes."

Hours of agony. Not something to look forward to.

As we stood outside the entrance, Derek appeared

out of thin air ten feet away, accompanied by a man and a woman, whom I could only assume were the witch and warlock Sofia had mentioned, Corrine and Ibrahim.

Their eyes rested briefly on me, and then focused on Ben. Corrine moved forward and drew him in for a hug, while Ibrahim patted him on the back.

"Welcome home, Ben," Corrine said, eyeing him anxiously. She was holding a canvas bag in one hand that was bulging with something. "I think it's best that we don't talk about this too much." She rested the bag on the ground and began pulling out vial after vial of red liquid that could have only been blood, laying them out on a nearby rock. "Let's just give you the cure as soon as possible so you can stop being such a threat to our humans, and then we can talk about the next step."

"That is a lot of immune blood," Ben said, eyeing the vials on the rock.

"We don't want anything going wrong," Ibrahim said. "There is something different about you, and we can't afford to take any risks."

"We're going to make you down twenty times the usual dosage that a vampire would take during the cure," Corrine said.

"Twenty times?" Ben said, taken aback. "Okay."

"And this is pure immune blood," Ibrahim added. "Not mixed with animal blood."

"Why would it be mixed with animal blood?" I couldn't help but ask.

Ibrahim turned to me. "To make our supply last longer and not keep having to draw blood from our resident immune, Anna, we figured out how to filter in animal blood while still maintaining the same effect. We kept aside just a small supply of pure blood…" He looked back at Ben. "And it's a good thing we did. Don't waste a drop, Ben. This stuff is precious."

Ben eyed the blood. "Okay."

He moved near the rock, and, opening all the bottles, began downing vial after vial of the blood. Once he was finished, he breathed out in satisfaction. Then Ben moved toward the Pit's entrance.

"Good luck, Ben," Derek said, looking at his son with trepidation. It looked like he wanted to draw him in for a hug, but he remained standing apart from him.

"Thanks," Benjamin murmured.

His mother gave him a tight hug, and then his sister.

Ben turned to face me, his bright green eyes looking deep into mine. Butterflies erupted in my stomach as his hands rested around the back of my neck and he dipped down to press his lips against mine. That he should kiss me so openly in front of his family made the blood rise in my cheeks.

"Good luck," I whispered.

CHAPTER 29: BEN

As I stepped inside the Pit, the sun blazed down on me like a thousand knives. The brightness was blinding as I staggered into the center of it. I'd felt the sun on me before, but in this small enclosure, it felt hotter than I'd ever experienced.

Every fiber of my being screamed to rush back out to safety, to the cool darkness. But I had to go through with this. There was no other way.

I focused my mind on stepping out again in a few hours as a human. All of my bloodlust problems solved.

Feeling normal again around my father and all the other humans I held dear. No longer feeling like an uncontrollable beast. Feeling myself again.

As much as I tried to focus on the end, there was just no way to ignore the burning in my flesh.

Although it was normal to feel pain like this when turning back into a human, part of me kept panicking that something was going wrong.

I did my best to remain silent, and not groan or make a sound. It would only make the experience more torturous for my loved ones standing outside.

The pain soon brought me to my knees, and I crouched on all fours, panting and drawing deep breaths, trying to find some way to not lose my mind.

I'm going to make it through this.

I'm going to make it through this.

I tried to distract myself with the thought of River, standing and waiting for me on the other side. I tried to lose myself remembering what it felt like to kiss those soft lips of hers, to run my hands along her curves, and look down into her gorgeous eyes.

That helped more than anything, but it still wasn't

enough to bring me relief.

I heard them calling for me, but I couldn't focus on their words. They entered my ears mangled and disjointed, and I could barely make sense of them.

Hours passed.

My skin felt like it had been deep-fried in a pan of oil and then scraped off with a carving knife, but my vision was too blurred to see the true state of it. I had lost my sense of touch temporarily. Although I ran my fingers along my arms, I couldn't sense what I was feeling other than the pain that spread throughout my entire body.

Lying on the floor, my eyes shut tight, I was no longer able to summon the strength to even move an inch. My throat was so dry and parched, it felt like I'd just swallowed a mouthful of nails.

Finally, the entrance swung open. Someone hovered over me—perhaps more than one person—and then the next thing I knew, my body lurched and I had been vanished out of that blazing hell. I landed on a soft mattress.

Opening my eyes, I felt my vision slowly returning. I

was looking around a cool, dim chamber in the Sanctuary. My parents, my sister, Caleb, River and the two witches stood around my bed.

"Benjamin."

I began to regain my sense of hearing. It was Corrine speaking. She touched either side of my face, and then my arms, my chest.

"Benjamin." It was my mother this time. "Can you hear me?" She spoke slowly, enunciating every syllable.

The back of my throat twinged painfully as I tried to speak. So instead I just grunted.

Bunching up the sheets between my fists, I managed to find the strength to sit up against the pillows and look around the room I was in. River, who was standing right next to my head, placed a hand over mine.

I looked down at my hand.

Its color was tinged red, but it was still unmistakably pale.

Can a human be this pale?

"Benjamin," Corrine said, her eyes wide with worry. "You are still a vampire."

I almost choked. Before I could respond, she held up another vial full of blood and tipped it into my mouth. The sweet immune blood trickled down my throat like honey, and every part of my skin began tingling.

I found my voice again. "What do you mean?"

"I mean you're still a vampire," Corrine said.

I looked at myself in the mirror fixed on the other side of the room. The rest of me was pale, just like my hands and arms. Opening my mouth, I bared my fangs. Then I flexed my claws.

"But... this is impossible," I gasped. "Remaining a vampire all that time beneath the sun... How could I have? I should've died."

"I have no clue," Corrine said. "Like you say, there's no reason for you to still be alive now. Your skin was reddish and blotchy just now before the immune blood healed you, but you endured nowhere near the damage you should have done as a vampire beneath the blazing afternoon sun for all those hours... You should be dead."

I'm still a vampire.

No, this cannot be possible.

"But you gave me a ridiculous dosage of immune blood. How could I not have turned? Sh-Should you have given me more?"

There was a pause, everyone in the room eyeing me nervously.

"I've a feeling," Corrine said slowly, "we could have given you all the immune blood in the world, and you still would not have turned."

CHAPTER 30: DEREK

It was a mystery to all of us. Not only Ben's inability to turn, but how in hell he was still alive.

I recalled my failed attempt to turn into a human while The Shade was under attack from the witches. If I had not been saved from the Pit by my wife, I would've died. My body had been scorched black after just a few hours. I had not been in there nearly as long as Ben. And yet here he was—although he had clearly been in agony, his body had been hardly covered with more than a few red patches.

It was deeply unsettling that not even Corrine or Ibrahim had a single clue as to why.

Benjamin looked shell-shocked as he sat back down on the treatment bed, staring blankly at Sofia and me. Despite the fact that Sofia and I had done what we'd thought was right for him at the time, I couldn't help but feel the guilt welling up within me again. I was the one who'd turned him. Ultimately, I was the reason he was going through this torment.

As Benjamin's eyes fixed on me, his expression changed. It was an expression I knew too well, not just from myself, but from other vampires when bloodlust was taking hold of them.

His facial features darkened, his eyes growing dull and blackish. The failed cure had drained him, and now he was starving for blood.

Although Corrine had just fed him a vial of immune blood, that would have soothed his throat, but it would not have even begun to satisfy the craving that was now roaring in his stomach. If anything, the exquisite taste of the immune blood would have just aggravated his appetite.

"He needs more blood," Corrine said anxiously. "But we can't afford to keep giving him pure immune blood."

River moved closer to Ben, pressing a wrist against his face.

"Leave it to me," I said, clenching my jaw.

Sofia shot me a confused glance. "How are—"

"I'll be back in an hour," I said firmly.

It was time that I stepped out of the room anyway. It was bad enough Ben just being on this island. Me standing in such proximity to him was unnecessary torture. I left the chamber, closing the door behind me, and then left the Sanctuary completely. Emerging in the moonlit courtyard, I hurried forward, my legs speeding me toward the Port. Arriving at the jetty, I walked along it and stopped at the end.

I stared out toward the ocean, past the boundary, until my eyes rested on the five gray hunter ships.

Now that it was amply clear that Ben could not turn back into a human, we needed to satiate him. Even with River standing next to him, diffusing the smell of human blood, there was only so long he could starve himself of blood before even her scent would not be enough to stop him from going on a rampage.

I shuddered, knowing my son's tendencies so well. I had been like him, albeit not such an extreme case. Although I despised it, even I had been able to drink animal blood if I forced myself.

As I continued to stare out at those gray ships, I knew that Sofia would not approve of what I was about to do. But right now, I couldn't bring myself to care. I had to do what was best for our son.

Besides, these hunters' presence was still annoying the living daylights out of me. I might've promised not to unleash an all-out war on them, but there was at least something I could do to take out my frustration.

But first, I needed to get help.

***

About ten minutes later, I found myself standing outside the mountain cabin of Shayla, a short witch with large eyes and a rounded face. She stood in her doorway, eyeing me curiously.

"What brings King Derek to my cabin?" she asked.

"I need help with something." Normally, I would have asked Corrine or Ibrahim first, but they were too busy with other matters now. "Magic us both to the Port and I'll explain," I said, before she could ask further questions.

She did as I requested, and as we stood at the end of the jetty, staring out toward the hunters' ships, I explained my plan to her. She looked doubtful, but agreed to go along with it.

After casting an invisibility spell over us, she transported us both outside of the boundary and made us hover above the water next to the ship that was furthest away from our island.

I peered through the windows near the base of the vessel as she moved us from room to room. I was looking for a kitchen, or somewhere a fire could feasibly be started…

I found what I was looking for as we reached the sixth window along. A kitchen area, filled with steel tables. One large gas hob was in the center of the room, atop which were four steaming pots. There was nobody inside.

Shayla and I couldn't make the mistake of going on board again, lest we trigger another alarm, but having the witch here with me meant that we could do a lot from outside.

"Are you thinking what I'm thinking?" Shayla whispered.

"If you're looking at the stove, then I think so," I said.

"Okay…" Shayla breathed.

A moment later, Shayla had used her magic to cause the sound of an explosion. Then, manipulating the fire beneath one of the pots, she made it blaze and begin rising upward toward the ceiling. It spread rapidly throughout the room.

The fire alarm went off.

A few moments later, a man dressed in black came hurrying in with a fire extinguisher. As soon as he neared the flames, Shayla filled the room with a thick smog that would impair any surveillance cameras' lenses.

The rest of the task was fairly simple. Shayla silenced

the hunter with a spell, and then vanished him out of the burning room, making him reappear outside beside us, invisible.

She transported the three of us quickly to The Shade, and as we arrived back on the jetty, she removed the invisibility spell. I gripped the hunter by the neck and forced him to the ground.

Although the conscience that Sofia had instilled in me was disapproving of what I was about to do, in that moment, it was the old Derek Novak that took over. The Derek Novak that was numb to loss of life. The Derek Novak that struck fear in every hunter's heart.

CHAPTER 31: BEN

In between the pangs of unbearable hunger ripping at me, the revelation echoed in my mind over and over again:

I can't turn back into a human. I am stuck as a vampire.

I grimaced at the bitter irony of it all. I'd wanted so badly for the cure to work so that I would stop craving humans. Now that I had taken the cure, I just found myself landed with ten times the desire to kill.

I could hardly look at River. I didn't want to see the

disappointment in her face. We had both been hoping so hard that this would work, that I would no longer need to rely on smothering her twenty-four hours a day. I hated to chain her to me like this, and I hated to be a burden.

Meeting her eyes was painful. I felt ashamed of what I was.

Although she'd stood by me, she knew what happened when she left my side. She had witnessed me slay three innocent humans back in the Egyptian guesthouse. She knew that I would do the same again the moment I got the chance.

A hushed silence filled the room after my father stepped out. I had no idea where he was going to get human blood from. I didn't want to think about it. I just needed the blood. And I needed it now.

Even River's presence was beginning to lose its effect on my craving. Each moment that passed, the smell of humans on the island was stronger in my nostrils. More tantalizing. More delicious.

When my father finally returned, he was accompanied by Xavier. My father held a steel bucket in one hand, containing blood that I could sense was warm even without touching it. I leapt from the bed and practically grabbed it from him. I drank directly from the bucket, hardly stopping to draw a breath as I swallowed gulp after gulp. I tried not to waste a drop, but I was shaking from thirst. Some ended up streaming down the sides of my mouth and onto my chest.

It felt like I was pouring water over a fire. By the time I finished, I felt calmer.

Sitting back on the bed, I looked over at Xavier. He gave me a weak smile, even as his eyes were filled with concern.

I wished I could've seen my aunt too, but I was glad they hadn't entered with her. She was a pregnant human. If I had done anything to harm her, I wouldn't have been able to live with myself.

The room fell silent again, all of us apparently lost for words. But all of us, I was sure, were wondering the same thing:

Where do we go from here?

CHAPTER 32: RIVER

I was still recovering from the shock of Ben's failed turning. He and everyone else had seemed so confident that it would work, and after seeing the amount of immune blood, which was supposed to be the key to making the cure work, I'd also been certain that he would step out as a human.

The plans we had made were crushed into dust. Now I didn't even know if I dared to leave the island, leaving him stranded with his cravings. I supposed I could leave him my blood, but I had already seen that did not always work.

I was sure we were all relieved when Ibrahim finally broke the silence.

"Obviously we have a lot to reconsider… In the meantime, why don't Corrine and I look at those tattoos you've got?"

I rolled up my sleeve, baring my skin for Ibrahim to look at, while Corrine examined Ben's arm.

At first I'd been scared to see Corrine so close to Ben. I'd thought that he might crave her blood too, but even I could sense that their blood was different to a human's. It was more bitter, and I could understand why it was not appealing to a vampire. At least not the way a human's was.

Now that we had been stumped in our plan, I was grateful for the change of subject before we returned to the inevitable. We needed something to break the tension.

Ibrahim and Corrine looked at Ben's and my brands. Their expressions were almost identical—deep-set frowns as they looked closely at the etchings. And then something flickered in the witch's eyes all of a sudden. Alarm. She seemed to have realized something that even the warlock hadn't yet.

He eyed her, raising a brow. "What? What do you see?"

She didn't reply as she left Ben and moved toward me, reaching for my arm and staring at the tattoo. As she examined my brand, the same alarmed look was in her eyes.

My breathing quickened as the blood drained from her face.

"What?" several of us asked at once.

Corrine just bit her lip. And when she finally did raise her face to make eye contact, there was an unmistakable look of terror in her eyes.

She uttered only two words:

"Oh, dear."

CHAPTER 33: BEN

The witch's look of fright and her refusal to give us even the slightest of explanations was eating away at my nerves. No matter how much we all pressed her, she refused to give us an answer.

"Not until I'm certain," she said, her hands trembling slightly.

"And when will you be certain?" I asked, no longer able to hide the frustration in my voice.

She didn't reply to my question as she walked toward the door. She just said, "Both of you stay in this room until I return."

She slammed the door shut, and we all stared at each other.

As per Corrine's order, we remained in that room for the rest of the day. When she still had not returned by the evening, even Ibrahim looked perplexed.

"River and I should return to the submarine for the night," I said. "I shouldn't sleep on the island."

Ibrahim shook his head. Then he glanced at my parents, who were still waiting with us in the room. "Derek, Sofia, I suggest that you two return to your penthouse for the night. I will stay here with River and your son. Corrine told them to wait here, and they should obey her. Even I'm not sure what that woman is thinking, but I know Corrine. When she gets into a mood like this, she should be listened to."

Ibrahim shot me a look as I was about to object again to staying on the island. "I will sit in that chair by the door and make sure both of you remain here. So you need not fear going on a rampage in the middle of the night. I will put a curse on you if I have to, but you will be all right so long as I'm watching you."

"All night?" I asked.

"All night," Ibrahim replied.

My parents bid us good night, albeit reluctantly, and left the room.

Ibrahim dragged an armchair over to the door. Since this room was windowless, there was no way I could exit without him knowing. Although the bed I was lying on was narrow, I moved up until my back was against the wall, so River could lie sideways next to me. It still pained me just to look at her. Once she had positioned herself on the bed, she reached up to touch my face, brushing my cheek with her fingers.

"We will figure something out, Ben," she said, even as I could tell that she held little conviction in her words. "I know we will."

I couldn't find it in myself to respond. I just nodded stiffly.

She wrapped her arm around me, holding me firmly, and then rested her head against my chest. She closed her eyes. Judging by her breathing, it took a long time for her to fall asleep, but finally her grip around me loosened a little and she nodded off. I remained holding her as I stayed awake deep into the night.

I had no chance in hell of sleeping. I just fixed my eyes on the clock in the corner of the room, watching the hours pass, my vision slightly unfocused as my mind was elsewhere, reliving the previous day's events.

I replayed every moment in that Pit back in my mind, every torturous moment, as if in doing so I might discover some detail that could tell me why I was trapped as this beast. As 2am struck, I sensed that even Ibrahim had fallen asleep.

My mind drifted unwillingly toward all the humans who would be tucked up in their beds tonight in the Vale. How easy it would be to smash through their windows and drink to my heart's content. I shook myself, forcing myself out of the ghastly fantasy.

Almost the moment I did, noises of The Oasis surrounded me, occupying my hearing so fully I was aware of no other sound. It had been a while since those noises had been accompanied by that strange voice, but now that also echoed around my head again.

The voice started softly, as it often did, then grew louder and louder, until it was hard to believe that the whole room was not ringing with the sound.

"Come back, Benjamin Novak. We know who you are, and we know what you want."

Usually the two lines were repeated one after the other, as if they were a verse. But this night, after the first echo, the voice began repeating only the last line, as if the first line had been forgotten.

"We know who you are, and we know what you want…"

Over and over again until I began to feel nauseous from the words.

Just as I was about to groan in frustration, something else arrested me.

While I was used to a wall of sounds closing down around me, I'd never had my vision hijacked.

This night, I did.

The room surrounding me disappeared and was replaced with a scene so strange, I wondered if I had indeed finally fallen asleep. But I didn't feel like I was sleeping. No. Something, or someone, was imparting a vision…

A cloaked figure stood in the center of a veranda

surrounded by giant broad-leafed trees and sheltered by low-hanging branches. Her long curly hair and the way her body curved betrayed her to be a woman, though she was anything but human. A set of wings were folded beneath her cloak and as she turned her face to the side, she revealed a black beak with a razor-sharp edge where her nose and mouth should've been. And instead of feet, she possessed talons.

She was a Hawk.

She stood looking down upon a wooden cradle. After watching it for several moments, she stooped down and reached into the crib. When she straightened again, she was carrying a dark-haired infant, wrapped in a blanket and deep in slumber. Then she spread her mighty wings and launched into the sky.

She rose higher and higher toward the canopy of leaves. Cradling the baby in her arms, she didn't stop until she had pierced through the leafy roof and burst out into the open sky, where an orange sun had almost set on the horizon.

Her wings beat heavily, speeding up as she soared over a jungle populated with gargantuan trees.

Even still, the baby slept.

Once the sun had bowed to the moon, the woman's flight had taken her beyond the forested landscape, and she had reached an ocean. There seemed to be a time lapse as the view changed beneath her several times. Although she flew over mostly water, exotic islands, desert terrains and lush valleys also passed beneath her.

Finally, she let up her speed when the clear sky gave way to thick clouds. She flew right through them, everything blurring as she navigated through the fog. Perhaps hours passed, it was hard to say for certain, but when the clouds got a little thinner and she lowered in altitude, the Hawk and the baby were flying over a landscape unlike any they had passed so far.

They were looking down upon a vast range of black mountains that stretched out as far as they could see. There was not a hint of vegetation in sight, nor any other life for that matter, just miles upon miles of shades of black and grey. It appeared that they had left the sun behind, yet the sky, which was filled with dark clouds, had an eerie reddish tinge.

A strong wind swelled up, forcing the woman to battle against it until she touched down on the peak of a mountain. Her talons gripped the rocks as her wings folded behind her back. Her long hair was a tangled mess as she adjusted the baby in her arms. Her eyes fell on a wide crater about ten feet away from where she stood. She moved toward it, and stopped at the very edge.

Staring down into it, she let out a piercing shriek.

Then she stepped back and fixed her eyes directly above the crater.

"I have the child," she said, her voice low. She remained staring into empty space.

A breeze blew against her, catching the edge of the baby's blanket and lifting it right off to unwrap the infant.

The infant levitated from the arms of the woman and began to float in midair, toward the center of the crater.

Its small fists clenched and eyes shut tight, still, the infant slept.

A thin veil of reddish mist manifested, and began to swirl around and around the infant. As it gathered speed, it became denser and denser until the mist turned into thick smoke and enveloped the baby completely. The woman watched, her narrow eyes fixed unblinking on the scene unfolding before her.

As the smoke billowed, gradually, it began to thin

again… until there was nothing left but the light reddish mist that had first touched the infant.

Leaving the center of the black crater, the baby floated back into the woman's outstretched arms. She looked the child over, then wrapped him again in a blanket.

"Is that all?" The woman spoke to some invisible force.

The answer came as a bone-chilling hiss:

"Take him back to Aviary… His time will come."

The vision disappeared as suddenly as it had shrouded me, and I sat bolt upright, almost sending River rolling off the narrow bed and falling to the floor. My chest heaved as I panted, trying to make sense of what I had just seen.

"Ben?" River whispered, clutching my arm. "Are you okay?"

I barely took in her words as my hearing was hijacked once again by the strange whispery voice for what would be the last time that night:

"We know who you are, and we know what you want…"

CHAPTER 34: JERAMIAH

Looking up and down the length of the dark island's shoreline, The Shade was more spectacular than I could have imagined.

While Amaya and I had been waiting outside the boundary for Benjamin and River's arrival at The Shade, I had wondered something that I had wondered many times before. Did The Shade truly live up to its hype?

Keeping the two of us invisible as we hovered over the waves, Amaya had landed us on the back of the submarine just as it entered The Shade's border. When we arrived inside, any doubts were proven unjustified.

Amaya transported us to the nearest beach, where I began my tour of the island. I didn't want to miss any part of it, and so I took my time. My witch companion might have been annoyed at the speed we were traveling if we had been in any other place, but even she appeared enamored by The Shade. I didn't hear a single complaint out of her, not that she had a right to grumble anyway—she owed me a favor.

We were careful to avoid people as we traveled by foot—although The Shade was so large and spread out, it was not difficult. I was fascinated by how varied the landscape was. There were not only lush forests, filled with giant redwood trees, but also fields and meadows where crops were being grown, despite the lack of sunshine—something that could have only been the work of a witch. There were also lakes, and the part of the island that we had not gotten to yet—far in the distance on the opposite side, the great mountain range.

As we walked along a particularly wide path through

the woods, I finally noticed what I had been dying to see since I arrived. Craning my neck upward, I found myself staring up at magnificent treehouses. The Residences. I had heard that was what they called this part of the island. They had once been home only to The Shade's Elite vampires, but now it appeared that many more vampires resided here. As I gazed up at the penthouses, I couldn't help but wonder which my father might've once inhabited…

Sensing Amaya less than a foot away from me, I whispered to her, "Wait here by this tree. I'll be back in a bit."

Stepping away from her, I launched into the air, aiming directly upward for the nearest veranda to me. Climbing up over its railing, I looked around, admiring the gorgeous residence up close.

Careful not to creak any of the floorboards, I walked silently toward one of the windows and peered inside. I found myself looking into a spacious living room. A dark-haired woman with blue-violet eyes sat in an armchair, a mug of steaming liquid clasped in one hand. I could tell in an instant that she was a human, and as my eyes lowered from her pretty face to her stomach, I realized that she was pregnant.

A human inhabiting The Residences? Strange.

It seems that much has changed in recent times.

Watching the woman for a few moments longer as she continued sipping from her drink, I left and moved toward the next penthouse along. I had to be more careful here not to be noticed. A couple sat around a small table on the veranda. Both of these were vampires. The man had red hair and a rounded, freckled face, while the woman had short black hair with an odd blue streak. As I listened in to their conversation, I gathered that the man's name was Gavin. I didn't care to stay longer to find out the woman's name.

Moving on to the next penthouse, I peered through the windows of each of the rooms until I spotted a spectacled man—also a vampire—bent over a pile of books. He was in a study of sorts, and in one corner of the room was a massive black dog, apparently asleep.

I passed by several more penthouses before returning to the ground and arriving at the tree where I had left

Amaya.

Sensing her proximity, I reached out and closed my hand around her arm.

"Let's continue," I said.

As we passed through the woods, our next stop was the Vale. Again, I found myself amazed at what they had managed to build here. Right in the center of this supernatural island was a bustling town filled with humans going about their lives. The Vale appeared to have almost been designed to feel sheltered from the rest of The Shade. The buildings were very differently constructed, and in general the architecture made it feel almost disjointed from the rest of the island. I wasn't sure if that had been done intentionally, or it was just how it turned out. It seemed in any case that these humans felt very much at home.

My mouth salivated as I caught sight of a group of pretty young women chatting by a fountain. I tore my eyes away from them, and Amaya and I continued forward.

Once I felt I had gained a good enough understanding of the town, we returned to the forest path and continued in the direction of the mountains.

Walking on in silence, I recalled Nuriya's warning to me before I left. She'd said that I wasn't to harm Benjamin or River. I smiled to myself.

What interest would I have in harming them anyway?

They weren't even alive the day my father was murdered.

But there were plenty of other people on this island who had been alive that day… It was a simple question of observing long enough to discover who was who.

As we reached a clearing at the foot of a mountain, voices echoed toward me from one of the forest paths. I stopped Amaya in her tracks. I stood deadly still, not wanting even the slightest crunch of leaves to interfere with hearing what they were saying.

A redheaded man and a blonde curly-haired woman stepped out into the clearing. I barely breathed as I listened to the conversation.

"I'm not sure that Ben would appreciate more visitors now," the man said. "Not after what just happened. As much as I'm dying to see him, I'll wait a bit longer."

"I think it's probably a good idea," the woman replied. "I can't imagine how devastated he must be feeling right now."

The man's face turned ashen. "Neither can I. I'm just not sure what on earth the next step can be. Even him leaving the island again, which Sofia suspects he will do... I mean, where would he go? And what would he do? Just hanging around outside The Shade isn't going to solve anything."

By now they had reached the foot of the mountain. They began making their way up a jagged staircase that was etched into the side of the rocks. They were silent for a while as they headed toward a wooden cabin, but just as they reached the steps leading up to it, the woman stopped. Reaching her arms around the man's neck, she planted a kiss on his cheek

"I know we will find a solution, Aiden," she whispered. "I just know it."

Aiden.

The name rang a bell.

A very loud bell.

Could that be Aiden... Claremont?

His next words confirmed my suspicion beyond all doubt. "It's just… so hard to see my grandson suffer so much."

"I know, my love," the woman replied gently. "I know."

As they climbed to the top of the steps and entered what appeared to be their home, the man's words played in my mind.

Aiden Claremont.

Grandfather of Benjamin Novak.

Father-in-law of Derek Novak…

Murderer of Lucas Novak.

READY FOR THE PENULTIMATE BOOK IN BEN & RIVER'S STORY?

A Shade of Vampire 19: A Soldier of Shadows
is the penultimate book in Ben and River's series as we
move toward the heart-pounding finale in book 20!
A Soldier of Shadows is available to order now.
It releases October 25th 2015.

Please visit www.bellaforrest.net for details!

Also, if you'd like to stay up to date about Bella's new
releases, please visit: www.forrestbooks.com, enter your
email and you'll be the first to know.

a soldier of shadows

A Shade of Vampire, Book 19

BELLA FORREST

Made in the USA
San Bernardino, CA
31 October 2015